>d>o>c
lust letters

> paul beckford
> and kevin dax

>d >o >c
lust letters

> The real-life e-mail romance
> of two cock-hungry man-sluts

>green candy press

d.o.c. lust letters

by Paul Beckford and Kevin Dax

ISBN 1-931160-03-1

Published by Green Candy Press

www.greencandypress.com

Cover and interior design: Ian Phillips

Cover photograph: Raymond Yino © 1999 Blue Door Productions, Inc.

Printed in Canada by Transcontinental Printing Inc.

PAUL BECKFORD

GWM, 26, 6', 150 lbs, athletic, lean, light brown hair, blue-green eyes, very good looking, facial hair in flux, lightly hairy, graduate student, deceptively wholesome in appearance, interested in intense, exhibitionistic, transgressive homo-sex...

--- ---

KEVIN DAX

GWM, 36, 6', 160 lbs, slim, handsome, blue-eyed, brown-haired, clean-shaven, smooth upper body, hairy legs, misleadingly wholesome in appearance, professional, interested in humbling himself before sexy men--as many as possible--of any race or type... Kevndax@aol.com

--- ---

To the memory of Boyd McDonald, Scott O'Hara, and all other writers who have sought to tell the truth about sex between men; to Green Candy Press, for taking on this book, by no means a "safe" project, in any respect; to the friend and expert editor who immeasurably improved the text and resolved many problems; and finally to "Paul", my handsome and lovable correspondent. I congratulate him and "Aaron" for their several years now of marriage, and wish them a lifetime together of continued happiness.

--- ▶ ---

FROM: KEVIN
DATE: TUESDAY, MARCH 12, 1996

Paul,

Welcome home.

Don't worry, I won't turn into a stalker or anything, but couldn't resist writing you a note. Don't know which persona I like better: the green-eyed, erudite, Bataille-reading beautiful young scholar; or the sex-animal in the shadows who fucked my throat with his beautiful hard dick, who crammed his hand in my mouth, who took Tahoe Tom's load on his upturned tongue. They're both pretty great guys.

Hope you come back up soon. Goes without saying that you can stay here, without any obligation. Use the place as a base. Of course if you want to use your host, you know he'll be pleased. Perhaps I could arrange entertainments for you, from my widening circle of tops....

Good luck with your studies and the rest,

Kevin

--- ---

FROM: PAUL
DATE: TUE, MAR 12, 1996

Kevin,

I told you that I check my e-mail zealously! I was thrilled to see your note, and hope to keep in touch regardless of how soon I make my way up to Berkeley. Actually, spring break is coming soon....

I don't think you need to choose between my personas--my goal is to reconcile my sides into one sex-crazed, art and culture entranced kinda guy, but most of my academic friends have no idea as to what sorts of behavior get me off. I will remember our encounters at the

>d.o.c.

Steamworks VERY fondly, and look forward to their sequels.

I spent the evening last night reading different parts of your latest book. This morning I thumbed through the first, and enjoyed the
strong homoerotic subtext to your themes.

And thank you again for the hospitable way you and George
received me Monday morning. I had a terrific time talking with you
both over breakfast, and I could have spent many more days like
yesterday, stopping at cafés, pausing at astounding architecture,
alternately visiting Moe's Books and seedy porno shops and eating
great Japanese food. It was a truly perfect day, and I was sad to
see it come to an end.

Keep me in mind as you shoot your next load, and formulate a few
fantasies that we can enact in the near future. I love the way our bottom sensibilities became so compatible, and I was extra thrilled to
find someone as into exhibitionism as myself. I miss you already.

Take care, and keep in touch. Give George my love and thank him
once again for me.

Ciao,

Paul

--- ▶ ---

FROM: KEVIN
DATE: WEDNESDAY, MARCH 13, 1996
Hi Paul,

Loved your letter. Felt reassured that you too enjoyed our time
together, and that I need not be too self-conscious about my enthu-
siasm for you. That said, I had the idea today that I might use you
(or my idea of you, because I don't want to impinge on your time, or

make you read things you don't want to), as an ideal reader for an
informal Débauché's Diary. As I say, there's no obligation to read
this, and I certainly don't want you to write back when you have
your hands full with work. But I feel a need to put some of my real-
life whoring into words.

Answered an e-mail I received from a married guy in SF, in
response to my AOL posting. He calls immediately, must have been
online. 36, married with a kid, HIV-negative, wants his dick sucked.
Says he's muscular, hairy, good-looking, horny. Sounds NY Jewish or
Italian on the phone: gruff, sexy. Wants to know why I'm not
swamped with responses. (Because it's been running for a while? Who
knows?) We talk about schedules, he opts for getting in his car and
coming over immediately, through the rain. Coming up the front
path half an hour later, we trade the classic sidelong stare: is he as
good-looking as he said? Did I oversell myself? I give him my well-
brought-up cocksucker's expression: open, approving, willing. In
fact, he's no god, but a sexy bull-dog guy, 5'9", indeed muscular. I
usher him in, offer him something to drink, he declines. Two seconds of awkwardness, then I drop to my knees and nuzzle the crotch
of his jeans. There's something going on in there already. I push up
his shirt and rub my hands over his broad hairy chest, regrown
from being shaved. Undo his pants, get my mouth around the head of
his dick that tents up gray Calvins. Pull those down, gulp down the
hard-on that pops out of his drawers. With his pants around his
ankles, I reach my hands around to his hard, very round ass and
furry crack. He strokes my hair and shoulders--friendly, affectionate. After setting up a rhythm, I push him gently back so he sits on
the edge of the bed. Crouching, I can get all of his nice, average-

>3

sized cock down my throat, and can rub mouth and face into his big tight round balls. He lifts his hips and thrusts into my mouth. Long hypnotized moments of eating cock. He asks if I'm OK, I say should I go faster or slower, rougher or smoother? Do your stuff, he says. He makes approving noises. I look up from between his knees; his eyes are closed, head to the side. Asks how many loads I've had from one guy at one time before—I say three, but long ago. Says he'll go twice. Standing again, he guides my hands to his butt, so I pull him into me. Asks how I want it, in or out? It's your life, he says. I say in. He comes with his dick fully planted, base throbbing in my lips, hot stuff shooting down my throat. How many times I've felt this, but never tire of it. I take everything, draw up for a second to swallow, then bury his dick again. He convulses lightly. Finally I rest my face in his bush, breathing hard, holding him tight around the waist. But he doesn't cum again, because a distant door slams.

More e-mail today. Devon, a boy I sucked off once, and who has been sending me edifying Eastern-wisdom aphorisms, has responded to a dirty message of mine. We've talked enough to know each other's tastes. He loves sex with girls, but likes to get his cock sucked, and occasionally wants to be fucked. I had written him, in response to his quote from Sri Whosits, that I couldn't shake the mental image, the fantasy, of lying on my side, his cock plunging down my throat in response to another cock deep up his ass. He writes that though he's still hoping for a monogamous thing with his new girlfriend Peggy, he still needs to get off. I mail him, call him, he calls back, I go over.

Devon greets me at his place, barefoot, fine straight brown hair to the middle of his back. Cute face, saved from prettiness by a cockiness, a faint smugness, a cognizance of being tasty. And he is.

25, blue-eyed, fair skin, medium height, slender but very round and full in the shoulders, biceps, ass—a Tom of Finland little brother, a squeaky-clean hippie bi-boy. Bare studenty place: small shelf with new age spiritual books, a deck of tarot cards, lava lamp, incense, boom box with mellow alternative CDs, a framed image of Christ, nineteenth century sweetness-and-light tradition. He teaches yoga and sells massage. Complains of cumming in such copious amounts, and having to get off so often. In fact, he's exasperated with cum: the smell, the amount, the spots on the spread (or across the room, on the wall). He can't imagine relishing sucking cock or eating cum for the pleasure of it, though he adds that he'll suck dick (but not swallow) to give somebody else pleasure. A buddy's duty. I tell him his problem—copious cum—is my pleasure.

Down to work. He pulls over a chair, gives me a hard look. I'm on my knees again. His stomach is hard and smooth, with a pretty happy trail of chestnut hair that leads down from his navel. His jeans down, he's already hard. I do my best, but on my knees before him I can't get him all down. His dick, very long and stout, curves upward. The skin is taught and pink, the head only slightly bigger than the shaft. A graceful object in the hand. Something to marvel at, to place in the mouth, to judge again in heft and mass. I know he doesn't have much time, and his dick is too big, so I lapse into occasional laziness and jack him with my hand, only the head in my mouth, or my tongue pressed against the slit. Still seated, he lifts his globular little butt rhythmically, to half-fuck my hand and mouth, but he doesn't talk or touch me much. Sweat pours down the side of my face—how long since I've sweated this way? It's still winter after all. I rotate around him so I can lean over his right thigh from behind and finally get his entire joint down my throat, to the root. I wonder if teeth or bending troubles him, but he doesn't complain. I can jam him all the way in several times with long strokes, but fall back on hand work. He asks if I'm OK. I'm very happy, I say, flushed; my legs smart from kneeling and contorting. More sucking. Ultimately he wanks himself while I suck his fat compact balls. They disappear into his body with each stroke, then pop out again. My nose deep in his balls, he exudes a funk; maybe he's not always squeaky clean. With quiet snorts (roommates in the apartment) and a hand on my chin, he guides me to the head of his cock before climax. I suck and lick the head, ready. He tenses and my mouth fills with an amazing amount of jism. Acrid, like last time; he seems to keep cumming. His legs jerk. His hand presses the back of my neck. I slide my mouth, still full of cum, as far down his dick as possible. He's still cumming. I think I can feel with my lips and tongue the passage at the base of his cock pulsing with sperm.

Afterward he says again he doesn't get why anyone would be so into it, though he's glad for his sake that people (so many people) want to suck his cock. He has a date with Peggy tonight, won't be anxious to bed her. She's held out, on the rebound.

We'll see each other again, have a friendly rapport. He's definitely one who would be worth sending your way, one worthy of you. You see Paul you can act as a standard for me in that respect, too: who is handsome enough, sexy enough, to merit the ministrations, should it ever be possible, of Paul?

Please don't feel obliged to send me a long response to this. A recovering Catholic, I'll be miserable if it appears I'm being a nuisance. But I feel inspired to put these stories (which are absolutely true) into text. We'll see if I get too lazy or harried to keep it up.

Or if I will be as honest with liaisons that are awkward and unpleasant, as I have been with today's, which went so well.

In any event, till next time, as Voltaire once signed a letter,

I kiss your cock,

Kevin

--- ▶ ---

FROM: PAUL

DATE: WED, MAR 13, 1996

Kevin,

Use me as you like--I LOVE reading about your debauches. I sit here with a hard-on after having read about your encounters and so wish I could have seen you, on your knees, sucking rods and tasting cum. Had I been on my knees at your side we would have kissed one another and coated each other's tongues in jiz again.

Unfortunately, my day consisted of mere jack off sessions, but you appeared in both--there'll be a third before I settle down to bed tonight. I thought about hitting the restrooms in the old P.E. men's room on campus where the last two stalls share a HUGE glory hole that's been hacksawed into the divider that separates them, but I always tend to see the same three guys there, and after a night at baths with you, my cock, my hand, Tom of Tahoe.... it just wasn't the same. I'm still reeling from this weekend. I'm still missing you.

So many times on Monday I wanted to stop you and take you down an alley, a stairwell, behind a building and embrace you, lick your neck, your mouth, suck your fingers, caress your cock and balls.... I wanted so badly to get it on with you in the backroom of the baseball card/comic bookstore while pimply-faced teenage boys

>7

watched us from another room.

I don't believe in cosmic shit, but I feel as though you and I are so alike in the ways we conceive life, love, sex, work--and I only care about you more when you tell me about your sucking off married men and too-butch boys with girlfriends. Thank god for those of us who volunteer to be the cum depositories for pent-up aching men. If only you were here, your opened mouth approaching mine, and cum dripping onto my tongue....

In between j.o. sessions with the mag I bought and the one you gave to me, I turned to Jansen and Gombrich to read about Le Vau and to see more depictions of his architecture. I imagined you next to me in France traveling from palace to palace, explaining his deployment of enfilades of doors and rooms.... Imagine what sacraments we could enact there, in public, with an audience, with Gallic versions of Tom of Finland slapping our asses, feeding us foreskin, bathing our faces with semen. In the name of the Father, the Son and the Holy Ghost....

Tell me more--make the posts as long as you want, as raunchy, as detailed. I'll be here, cock in hand, wishing I were watching and participating. We make a terrific team, if only virtually. Meanwhile, I'll think of you standing next to me--your left hand pulling my head back with a fistful of hair, your right hand gripping my chin, holding my mouth open. Your too-butch boy and your married-with-a-kid 5'9" man are standing side by side with hard cocks in hand taking turns with my mouth and throat. They grunt, and drip sweat into my eyes, the boy takes a leak in my open-mouthed face and his work-out piss drips from my chin to my own throbbing cock. They force both cocks into my throat at once--I suck, gag, lick their piss slits and savor pre-cum. I lick the ever-flowing ooze from their veiny shafts, and work their cocks into seething furies of cum before they toss their loads onto my cheeks, my eyes, into my hair, and onto my upturned-tongue-extended mouth. You look into my face and see ropes of jism dripping from my lips and teeth and down my throat before you put your own dripping cock into my mouth, I wrap my lips around it and you begin to unload your own thick mass into my gulping mouth. Stranger things have happened, you know....

Keep the fantasies cumming--and I'll be on the prowl soon so I'll have more material for you. Meanwhile, my most insistent fantasy is the one in which we perform together again. I can hardly wait. Be raunchy.

Love,

Paul

--- ▶ ---

FROM: KEVIN

DATE: WEDNESDAY, MARCH 13, 1996

Hey Tiger,

God I loved your letter. You surprise me, though, too. In the full light of day, in my goofy glasses, even as our new friendship grew, I thought your interest in having sex with me would have abated. I watched you, on the other hand, with some awe. Like all of the truly handsome among us, the harsher the light, the more your beauty stands out. I was grateful to you for wearing your robe to breakfast. Tried not to stare stupidly into those jeweled eyes of yours. I wish now I had sought out some alleyway or campus tearoom in order to get my mouth on you. And of course I was disappointed to let you leave town without feeding me your sweet load. Anyway, there will be other opportunities....

Thank you for your cum-dripping imagery. I wish you many horny university men, and hopefully not the same three glory hole guys. I know what that's like. If only the general run of men—straight and bi, I mean—would avail themselves more often of handsome and sportive cocksuckers like yourself. God knows they need it.

I can't shake the image of you at the baths, your beautiful face turned up, mouth open, tongue up, while Tom's fat cock head bobs ready to shoot in your mouth. Lots of cum, spurt after spurt. One of the guys watching gasps appreciatively. Then you rocked back on your heels, face dripping, mouth slightly open. Kissing some of the cum out of your mouth, rolling it between our tongues, is one of the hottest things I've ever done, at once incredibly tender and absolutely sleazy. I won't be able to rest until we've sucked, the two of us, another stud's cock. Or 12.

In the mean time, you're ever present in my thoughts. And now when I suck a dick I'm already writing about it for you in my head. And later I get to commune with you again by writing at my keyboard.

Further Adventures in Cocksucking:

So, Gary shows up after midnight last night. I'm disappointed: he's my age, which is not usually an impediment, but his looks and style are of a kind that suit a younger man. Styled hair, a little full, looking like a 60s-vintage portrait of Yves St. Laurent, or a young Nureyev. In fact, premier danseur, Slavic features: high cheek bones, arched brows, wide full-lipped mouth, ever-present Etruscan smirk. And a chatterer. We chat. He accepts a glass of wine, comments on the polar bears on TV (on to create background noises against snoozing husband). Wears too-tasteful gray dress shirt and

tie; works swing for a legal firm. He smells of eight hours in an
office: faint cologne, secondhand smoke—not entirely unpleasant.

I throw my face into his lap anyway, no real transition from
polite babble to rubbing my mouth on his crotch. Getting his clothes
off him brings pleasant surprises: soft, smooth skin wrapped around
very lean, well-proportioned muscles. Slender hips, broad chest;
could be an Attic Kouros' body, in the flesh. Huge dick, already
spongy hard, and big balls. Bemused sotto voce guffaws as I get most
of his cock in and out of my mouth. He rubs my head too much, lacks
macho restraint. His cock head in my mouth, I look up at him. He's
still smiling defensively, but he's turned on watching me suck him. I
am more and more into it. His dick is an enormous challenge. I never
ask anyone how big his dick is, even if I have it in my mouth. Seems
crass. But his must be 9", and very fat. Crouched in front of him—
it's not rock hard so I can make it bend slightly as it goes down—I
get it almost all the way down. Wrap my thumb and forefinger around
base of cock and balls; get my lips almost to the root. I get him to
lie back on the bed, then kneel before him and space out on the full-
ness in my mouth. I soften the interior of my throat and mouth so
that all surfaces, except teeth, hug his meat. I move to the floor and
lean over him from the side, and force his entire member down my
throat. A point of pride: yes, even this one I can get down. I've been
working with different rhythms, mostly late-night no-hurry pace.
Gary rotates his hips around and up to my face. At one point I ask
him to kneel on my chest. He looms above me, sticks half his dick in
and out of my mouth, pulls it out and slaps it lightly on my lips and
open mouth. I'm very happy in this position, pulling my own hard
dick, looking up at a distant, towering, classical body, a face that is

finally serious, my face full of cock. He manipulates himself, rubs his dick all over my face. I slide my mouth back and forth under his shaft, he grunts happily as I get both balls into my mouth.

He wants to come lying on his back. He jacks himself off while I lick spit all over his balls. They're big, but loose enough in their sack to push around pleasingly with my face. After an hour and a half of sex, he shoots on his flat belly. I'm pleased, and perfectly happy to forgo his load. I'm warmed to his huge joint and sculpted trunk, but I don't want to drink his cum. Because he's a dandy? Is this internalized homophobia? Who cares? He certainly doesn't expect me to take it, and assumes, as many guys do, that shooting on one's stomach is the way to go. This time, I agree.

We part cordially, with friendly hugs. I'm uncertain if I will want a reprise, but tell him: soon, anytime. I did end up, after all, happy to work on him. If we could put a mask on him, like the heroine's owl hood from the end of L'Histoire d'O, and keep him from prattling, he'd be a welcome addition to any orgy.

Much love,

Kevin

--- ▶ ---

FROM: KEVIN
DATE: THURSDAY, MARCH 14, 1996
Paul,

Hope you're well. Uncertain that you received my letter of yesterday, especially since I sent it a new way. Being lazy, I summoned up your letter after it had been retired to post office, then hit reply to send a new one. May not have gone through. When is spring break? Would love to have you back sooner rather than later, but we've also got a couple of batches of houseguests in coming weeks. Lemme know.

Whew, no sex on Wednesday! Rather a relief. My throat was getting a little sore, like the cervix of a friend of mine who complains about her young husband's generously proportioned member. Did however trade messages with two young guys.

At the risk of becoming tedious with my ongoing blowjob chronicle, I herewith bring you up to date:

Kenneth, one of the two, calls today and comes right over. Our second time. Jocular friendly connection. As his first message read: 6' tall, 160 lbs, lean, in shape, works out, goatee, brown hair and eyes. Also, as I found, punky in an appealing way: buzz cut and cap, both nipples pierced, a few small tattoos. Lean indeed, long tight body, furry chest. Funny voice too, very low, sexy and gruff, but with a speech impediment that suggests a tough little kid. Not classically handsome, but good-looking an butch-cute, joli-lad. All the more appealing because he's an out young queer, involved in SF alternative political/art stuff.

This time he came in and immediately began to strip. Both of us standing, he had his hands as much on me as mine were on him. My face in the hollow of his collarbone, loved moving my hand down his belly, around his balls, into his hairy crack, onto his firm small cheeks. He undid my ripped-to-shit cut-offs, grabbed my hard cock. I pushed him onto the bed and popped his half-hard dick into my mouth. Not very big, but big enough to chow down on. Big hairy balls hugging his body. Like last time, he fucked my mouth pretty fast, I moved my head as fast in response. Barely had to come up for air. Instead I was pleased that he got mostly mouth, rather than hands.

>13

Very hot to lock eyes with him while he pumped. Deeply satisfying to feel and hear him approaching climax. Just before he cums, I plant him fully down my throat and dilate and squeeze my throat muscles. He shoots and I cease moving, except for swallowing. He guffaws at my deep fast breaths as I pull off his dripping cock, and chuckles again as I murmur into his scrotum: thanks for your load, Kenneth. No man, thank you he says. We quietly joke about the symbiosis of it all. He says he'll call again soon.

Just an hour or two later, James calls. We'd traded messages. Berkeley grad student, 6'1", 190 lbs, good-looking. Utmost discretion necessary. With bike and helmet at the door, can't see him at first. Short black beard, pierced ears, sturdy, nice-looking, perhaps Jewish. Could be straight or gay or in between. Inside, he wants to give me a few words of preamble: mostly straight, but has had experiences with men. Not defensive about this, rather wants to show that he's game. Wants to protect his privacy, but likes the furtive aspect of personals ads. Likes to get blown, but has never come that way, which has frustrated at least one ex-girlfriend, who wanted him to cum in her mouth. Warns me that he's slow to get warmed up.

I want to get started. His pants are down, boxers too. Soft, his dick is already a nice size and lolls to the side. But I concentrate on his big dark balls. He makes very sexy sounds of approval, and his dick rouses itself. It's a hot day, and he's come by bike; he tastes of fresh clean sweat. I run my hands up to his broad slightly furry chest, fine black hairs spread across pale skin, he's wet. His dick becomes a handsome 7" or so, thick and uncut (so he's not Jewish!). Feels great to fuck him with my mouth, and I work on him for quite a while. I ask him to stand so he can watch us in the full-length

bedroom mirror. He pushes his hips into me, getting up a nice pace.
He lies back on the bed, I kneel in front of him. He kneels over my
chest as I lie on my back, fucks my mouth as I lie on my back,
crouches over me, pumping away as my head is pinned and my mouth
filled again and again. I lie on my side, he fucks my throat easily by
swaying forward and back. He asks if I like the way he fucks my face,
I answer with my mouth full. Different combinations again, but it is
with me on my side, deep-throating him, that he begins to get close.
I do my best, trying to keep the pace fast, steady and deep, but
choke at times and must take a breath and pump him with my hand.
Finally he announces that he's about to cum, and, as usual, I get his
whole length in me and take all his sperm. Thanks, he says. Hey
thank you. When we get up and dress, I ask him if indeed he has
never before shot during a blowjob, and that I'm honored. He nods. He
says he'll call me sometime, but that I shouldn't call him, he has a
straight roommate. I say I hope he does call.

   Your ever-hungry uncle,
   Kevin

--- ▶ ---

FROM: PAUL
DATE: THURS, MAR 14
Kevin,
I did get the first message (Wednesday's) you'd sent, but enjoyed
rereading about your midnight encounter. The two additions--today's
tricks?--were great as well. Sitting here with my fly open, my boxer
briefs hooked around my freshly shaved balls, and wishing once
again that we were nearer one another.

Last night I had my first S/M encounter. I've been curious to try this
for a while--just experimented with S/M and spitting (on my face while
I sucked) at a bath in Palm Springs last month, and I've been interested to know where my boundaries are--or do I have any? After watching a film at a friend's house Wednesday night, I go to Fairmount Park
where the cruising can be decent after dark. No luck and a cop car
chases the few of us away. I head to the fancily named Le Sex Shoppe
in downtown Riverside hoping for at least a quick encounter in a video
booth. I'm horny as hell, and your journal is only making me throb all
the more. Immediately, I make eye contact with a curly-black-haired,
moustached, shortish man--looks to be Jewish--wearing a leather
jacket and black suede Airwalks. Has to be at least ten years older
than me. I move to the booth next to his, and he keeps eyeing my ass,
walks over and runs his hand up and down my crack. I, of course,
respond favorably. He asks me what I'm into. I tell him sucking, being
fucked, and that I can get into lots more if he's interested. He perks up
and I tell him that I'd certainly be up for watersports. He's into leather
and wants me to come home with him. Sure I'm not too experienced
with the leather scene, but am willing to be trained if he's interested.

I follow Richard to his apartment in San Bernardino where he
immediately makes me a margarita (used to be a bartender), and asks
me to strip in front of him. I do, and he seems to approve. He guides
me to his bedroom and shows me the closet full of leather paraphernalia he's been accumulating. I'd already noticed the padded sawhorse with vises clamped to the legs in his dining room. He puts a
slave collar around my neck, a ball-separator and cock ring around
my balls and cocks and chooses a number of paddles--leather, stud-
ded and wood. He's REALLY into spanking and playing the daddy/bad-

boy scene, and he's not bad. He paddles well, producing just the right amount of noise without the equivalent amount of pain or damage.

But my ass is too hairy, and he asks if it would be OK to shave it. I've been wanting to for a while, so I'm game. He spreads a large bath mat on his long bathroom sink counter where I'm placed face down, ass high in the air and cheeks spread. He's drinking Bud trying to work up some piss, and every so often he pours some into my throat. He softens the hair on my rump and begins to rub it with shaving cream. He ends up shaving my ass smooth--it's already beginning to be red from the paddlings--as well as my crack, my hole, and my balls. He tells me to get into the shower, he goes back for my underwear and makes me put these back on. Keeps pouring beer down my throat, sometimes he fills his own mouth with it and then spits it onto my face and chest. He tells me to start pissing in my underpants; I concentrate and relax and soon I'm soaking my briefs in beer piss. As soon as I begin, he points his own dick at my face and starts pissing all over my face, my hair and down to my crotch. Of course, now I need to be spanked.

Being paddled on a piss-wet butt creates a pretty sharp sting, but I'd worked myself up into a frenzy of self-abnegating ecstasy. A buddy of his calls and wants to come over to watch some porno. 20 minutes later, I'm handcuffed and presented to his buddy who grunts approvingly at my beet-red hairless ass. The sawhorse comes out into the living room and I'm spread over the length of it with my wrists cuffed to the front legs and my ankles strapped to the back. More paddling (his buddy is only allowed to look, not touch) and then Richard starts to fuck me, riding me like a pony.

The buddy leaves; more paddling, more fucking, more piss. I'm

being a good boy. He says he'd like to have me come over and service four or five of his buddies--a fantasy I've had for years now. I
told him I would so long as they coated my open-mouthed face with
load after load of cum.

Richard doesn't get off because he jacks off in this really weird
and difficult way and I think he's been taking coke or something all
night long. I leave at six a.m. with a sore butt, but I still have a load
to release.

I drive up to Blue Cut Canyon--a place north of San Bernardino on
the old highway where men congregate and do it in the bushes. I
worry that it's too early, but I blow two men just after seven and
get fucked soon after that. He likes my welt-red ass. One of my
favorite face-fuckers shows up at about eight and we find a nice
spot where he can stand on a rock and I can blow him. He's a great
talker and has a short but immensely thick cock. He also oozes a
nice lot of pre-cum, which he loves to squeeze out the tip of his
dick and rub across my lips and face. I suck at my own pace and
preferred depth for a while, but he gets more exited and grabs the
back of my head, forcing me onto a cock that seems much longer
when he's thrusting than when I'm controlling the sucking. Brings
tears to my eyes and makes me gag like crazy. I'm sliming his cock
with spit and mucus, but he loves it. I'm feeling like the back of my
throat is beginning to be raw when he starts telling me he can feel
his load working up. I get more animated and he tells me it's rising,
it's rising. Soon he's pumping hot cum into me and it's dripping out
the corners of my mouth and onto my beard. Just the way I like it.

I head home and jack off to your e-mail before I fall asleep for the
next few hours. And now I'll reread your last post and jack off again.

I'd love to visit over spring break, but of course I'd need to work out some details. My last paper is due Thursday, March 21, and then school starts up again the first week in April. Sounds like this might be the time your company is in town. In any case, I always have Thursday through Sunday off this next quarter, and my only real (graduate) class meets Wednesday evenings. In other words, I could really take time out to visit just about anytime. Of course, please let me know if and when visiting is ever convenient and comfortable for you two. But you're always on my mind, and I long to be with you again--for all sorts of reasons.

Love and lust,

Paul

P.S. You should have seen the Polaroid Richard took of me (from the rear) strapped onto his sawhorse. Last night was a first for a lot of things.

--- ▶ ---

FROM: KEVIN
DATE: THURSDAY, MARCH 14, 1996, 10:00 P.M.
Paul,

What an amazement. It's a wonder you can get through your classes. No really, I am filled with admiration for your daring, gratitude for your account, and jealousy that I wasn't there to see you get all that cum and piss. And how I'd love to see that beautiful boyish ass of yours pounded by a big hand and then plowed by a hard cock. I love the hair on your body, the short light hair on your ass, but know that your pretty little hole (though I haven't properly studied it, or fucked it--yet--with my tongue) and round cheeks will look very fine hairless.

Please count on me for maintenance shaving in future. Thank you for
the mental images. Save that Polaroid. Perhaps I'll send some snaps of
my own--something I've wanted to do more of, more often

I hope your S/M top appreciates his good fortune in being able
to use and humiliate a young man as desirable as you. I hope he
comes through with a party, with you as the cake, the beautiful
soiled centerpiece of all their spurting cocks.

I thought I'd had enough of sex for a few days, what with sucking off my ad respondents, and then reliving it in the telling. But
you inspire me, and with the excuse of executing a few errands I'll
spend all afternoon and evening tomorrow at the Campus Theater in
SF, a truly sordid place, and will tell all.

Looks like the next week will be taken with houseguests, but I'm
delighted that your schedule will be so flexible. We'll work something out. My dick has been dripping all through your letter.

Much brotherly affection, drenched in jism,

Kevin

--- ▶ ---

FROM: PAUL
DATE: FRI, MAR 15, 1996
Kevin,
Unfortunately I don't have the Polaroid; I told Richard that if my face
appeared in it, it would have to be destroyed. Don't ask me why I'm
so paranoid about that--but he kept the photo. Maybe I can get
another made. And I'd love to see yours! If nothing else, I feel like I
need a snapshot of your beautiful face. If you could manage at some
point, I'd appreciate a photo of you--just something I can keep next

to my computer screen and linger over while I get hot and bothered reading your provocative posts.

I slept like a log last night. Today I've GOT to get some reading and research done, or I'll be in deep shit. So I don't think I'll be able to work in any sexual adventures. Of course, any tales of your sleazy dealings in SF could certainly change my mind....

I'm sitting here in my bathrobe thinking about sitting in your kitchen; continental-style breakfast of yogurt, fruits, nuts, tea; and terrific conversation with you and George. Wish we could have breakfast together now and then go off and roam the city some more. I love your passion for things both beautiful and base: art-books/pornography, fine architecture/the bathhouse space, your photography/your photography-as-lure, eating food/eating cum.

So when is your birthday? Where did you grow up? How did you meet George? I know that these are questions better asked face-to-face, but I'm hungry to know more about you. It's strange how we spent less than 24 hours together, and I already feel fiercely connected to you, and yet I don't have all that much actual information about you. Strange how knowing someone can happen without really knowing that much about a person at all. I can't believe how masterfully George was able to elicit my life story between walnuts and a second cup of tea.

Let me know if I ever get carried away in these letters. I feel as though I let my crush on you get the better of me at times, and I go off in ways that might make you feel uncomfortable. I've never swooned over a married man before, and I'm not sure of the protocol. In any case, reprimand me--cyber-spank me, if you will--when I spin out of control. Your letters on the other hand delight me to no end. I've been checking my mail on an average of three times a day. And I have a terrible time concentrating on my work! I should go and eat, read, get ready for this afternoon.

"I ate with you and slept with you, your body has become not / yours only nor left my body mine only."[1]

Yours,

Paul

--- ▸ ---

FROM: KEVIN

FRIDAY NIGHT, IDES OF MARCH

Paul,

The only thing that makes me uncomfortable about your wonderful letters and more wonderful sentiments is that I am not worthy of your affection, and that I am keeping you from your work.

As far as I'm concerned, you are an amazingly beautiful young man, brilliant and sexy. I, on the other hand, am quickly going to seed; occasionally impotent with men whom I find truly attractive; fixated on a narrow range of sexual expression. You, in your slut-tish bravery and breadth of sexual interest, are an inspiration. I admit that I am smitten with you, that I want to lick your cum off a filthy floor, that I want to guide fat slick cocks into your open mouth and tight hole, in twos and threes. I already love you.

The day's events:

Not a banner evening for sex, all in all. The Campus Theater was

----

1 Whitman, Walt. Leaves of Grass. Philadelphia: David McKay, [c1900]; Bartleby.com, 1999. www.bartleby.com/142/. [June 2001].

even more deserted than usual when I arrived at 3:30 p.m. Watched the various porn films on monitors spread around the place: big screen and stage upstairs in theater proper; downstairs in maze, stinking-couch rec-room, and bare bones "arena," three tiers of benches around a dimly lit wrestling mat. Let a few people suck me for a while, a little Filipino guy and a broad bear. Felt good, but neither gave me the kind of deep slow mouth that I wanted; instead they hoped to get me off fast. Finally shanghaied the only good-looking guy in the place: early 20s, tall, broad-shouldered, short-haired, handsome in a brooding way, like one of Donatello's big-headed prophets for the campanile in Florence. Classic stand-up foreplay, rubbing our hands up each other's shirts, down into the crack and crotch, licking each other's necks. I was just getting into swallowing his very big down-bending joint, working up a rhythm, when we were interrupted by an unappealing character who moved up on him from behind. My youth absented himself even though I quickly shooed away the intruder.

There followed lots of fruitless scurrying around, waiting for the place to fill up. Communed with a couple of go go boys during their shows, slipping them a dollar each time they came round. Danny, a studly Michelangeloesque 30-year old with a military haircut, liked the way I sucked his nipples and stroked his long, hard dick for several deep strokes. A singular honor. I'd seen him many times before, but I don't remember getting to blow him before. They're not supposed to entice you into a private show, where for 20 bucks they'll let you suck them, or whatever. Even so, certain dancers will sometimes let certain audience members suck their dicks when they come by. By the cruel rules of the unwritten homo code, cocks get

stuck into the mouths only of the younger and the relatively good-
looking guys. I have been lucky enough to count myself among this
group, at least in the not-very-exclusive Campus Theater demo-
graphics. I hasten to add that most of the truly young and handsome clients (scarce anyway) aren't as cock-greedy as I, and wouldn't
dream of doing anything more with these guys than running their
hands over them. Sometimes the tentativeness of these boys, or
married men, or tough, deprived characters, is truly affecting. The
nervous caress of a forearm that an uptight client gives a naked
performer can be sexier than my hand up his butt. So, in order to
suck go-go boy dick in public, it helps to be a slut. Since I end up
at this place once every month or two, the dancers recognize me,
and a few have honored me over the years by ramming their dicks
down my throat as soon as they get to me, however many tourists
from Topeka or Osaka are sitting around us.

One such fellow is Steven, who gave the 9:30 show on the main
stage. Huge, beautifully proportioned black guy. Big dick, big butt,
big chest, big jaw; a Marvel Comix kind of guy. Nice smile with a real
brain behind it. We were socially acquainted before we began our
performer-client relationship, but I don't think either remembers
how. Our exchanges now consist of my sticking a dollar bill in his
sock and him sticking his mammoth dick in my mouth. Again, in my
childish pride, I'm always pleased that I get such an unlikely object
all the way down. I was sucking away tonight when he leaned down
and said that he would reward me by climaxing with me. He stood
and led the way from the dark back row to the center spotlight,
where I took another seat while he jacked himself standing hard by.
As I stroked his thighs and chest, I told him I'd be willing to suck

him there in full view. Still wanking, he said that probable wouldn't be cool. Yet he was pumping right in my face, and then pushed his dick against my lips and tongue, fully lit by the spot. Too briefly, I rolled my tongue around the fat head. He withdrew and shot to applause, gave my shoulder a friendly squeeze before retiring.

Meanwhile, someone had cleaned out the unsecured locker filled with my stuff: my best (only presentable) sports jacket, leather bag with books and the (irreplaceable) disk of my last book. No hysteria, but plenty of dismay and self-recrimination. Such a dumb thing to do, and to lose something that important at a dreary dump that, for all of the forgoing juicy dicks, offered mostly nothing but hours and hours of anxious boredom. Talked to the brain-dead twinkie box-office boy, then the much more conscientious manager. Made the rounds with their flashlight. Nothing. Resignation. Manager himself (Stuart, sometime performer, has never let me suck him--not that he remembers me from one time to the next anyway) searches and finds everything, surprise, intact, in a dark corner. Presumably awaiting the right moment for thief to go through it or to spirit it away. I've lucked out again. A sign to waste less time? To whack off more often in the privacy of my own home? Or sign that the angels have forgiven me again for sniffing after penises in dank cellars, and that maybe they approve?

Now, if only the world were populated entirely with men like you, and cartoon character studs like Danny and Steven, I could get more work done at home AND more cocks sucked, at home and abroad.

Kevin

--- ▶ ---

FROM: PAUL
DATE: SAT, MAR 16, 1996
Kevin,
Just got back from campus where I watched a documentary on the
bringing down of Soviet propaganda monuments in the former USSR.
Lenin was a really attractive man.

My meeting with my prof. went well. I'm starting out with
Clarissa (thank God he's giving me three weeks on it) and from there
we do the Fielding siblings, Sterne, Edgeworth, and Wollstonecraft.
He's really giving me free reign on this one.

So what kind of underwear do you wear? I have a big thing for
underwear. As a child, I would lick the crotches of the men advertising white briefs in Sears catalogues. Also, when I was in Junior
High, I was often asked to baby-sit. I would find the men's underwear in clothes hampers and sniff at the crotches. I still love to nuzzle my nose into a man's underwear-clad groin, lick his cock and
balls through the cotton, and run my tongue under the waistband
and the hem at the legs before he takes them down. I've always had
the fantasy of receiving a pair of white briefs that were well deco-
rated with piss and cum stains…keep that in mind, will you?

My roommate is making dinner tonight, and we may end up going
dancing later. After X-Files of course. I got nothing accomplished
today. Hopefully tomorrow…. Hope your day in SF was successful.
Tell me ALL about it.

In perversity,
Paul

--- ▶ ---

FROM: PAUL

DATE: SUN, MAR 17, 1996

Kevin,

After X-Files with friends at Meg's (the leather-dyke--her chaps fit me), we all went out to Riverside's least pathetic gay bar, the V.I.P., to dance. A rude and tyrannical drag queen m.c. kept the music from playing until after one a.m.; there was some sort of underwear contest going on, but not a single contestant was the slightest bit enticing.

We get home at three a.m. and I have a phone message from the nude housecleaning service I do jobs for on a very irregular basis. It appears I have a job to do nine a.m. Saturday morning. This means I get four hours sleep, and have to drive out to Hacienda Heights on the outskirts of LA. I wouldn't do it, but I need the cash, so I wake up, shave, and confirm the appointment. I arrive at Joe's and he's a very old, very flabby, very pock-marked man--he looks tame and sweet, but I have to reconcile myself to the fact that I may have to choose what I will and won't do with him later. He wants me to clean his floors, so I strip and start on his tile and linoleum in the bathrooms and the kitchen, which are, of course, already immacu-late. He watches and talks to me: So do you like to be nude? Do your clients ever touch you? I've been learning how to massage.

I give him a pretty good view of my butt while I run the sponge along his floors. We work on his TV room together washing windows and dusting his shelves piled with porno-tapes and mags--as well as silk plants and photos of his parents. He strips and we talk more about his interests in nudism and massage. He's extraordinarily sweet, actually, and the poor thing really wants contact with other humans. He bought the house so that it would be comfortable for two, but that's never really worked out for him. He would like to massage other men, but they ask if he's young and has a tight body. He's started working out.

He asks if I've ever thought of doing massage instead of cleaning. I could make more money and it would be more fun. Do I want to see his massage tapes? I say sure and we go lay on his waterbed together. His tapes are about The Art of Sensual Touch--very silly and totally soft porn (no hard-ons) although the models are delicious. He asks if I've ever had a massage, and he begins to massage me, explaining to me what he's doing as he does it. Just giving me information. He's got a weird dick--uncut with lots of foreskin, huge piss-slit and very veiny, but it only springs into an erection sporadically. I decide I could massage him, so I start to rub his back and neck. He gives me pointers and tells me I could make a lot of money doing this if I wanted to. We spend about 40 minutes cuddling and rubbing one another. I think about his flesh and all the so-called "defects" that mark it. What does it mean that this sort of physique should repulse us? This man wants so badly to be naked with other men, and to touch them and be touched. It strikes me as very sad.

He asks if I want to see his massage table. He's very proud of it, but he doesn't get much chance to use it--he needs someone to practice on. I can come over whenever I feel like I'd like a massage, he says. I half think I might take him up on it, even though his are nothing like the two professional massages I've had in my life. He strokes my dick, and I tell him he'll make me cum if he keeps doing that. I cum all over my chest and belly, and he seems happy he was able to get someone else off. As I dress, he gives me §70 (§30 goes to the cleaning service), and once again he tells me I can call whenever I want to get a massage. I tell him OK. I know I'll probably never call.

I call a kid named Ted--I sucked him last quarter, and he called me a lot afterward, but for some reason I never returned his calls even though I'd thoroughly enjoyed myself. He's not home and a woman answers. I'll call him later. Richard, the S/M master of Wednesday night calls--he's off work, and wants to know if I'd like to keep him company tonight. I tell him I have plans. I'm just too tired, and I know that a sexual encounter with him would be simply too high maintenance. I check my e-mail; no message from you, but that's OK, cause I know one's coming and that you're probably off whoring around, thinking of me as a dick twitches in your mouth and the last spurts of cum hit the back of your throat. You're the tops.

So now I'm going to curl up with work and try and concentrate on finishing my second read of this novel before I go to bed tonight.

Have a good night. I'm so glad your stuff wasn't irrevocably lost. My heart stopped when I read about the loss of your manuscript disk, but the angels were obviously watching out for you--and approving of your every sleazy move.

Missing you,

Paul

--- ▶ ---

FROM KEVIN
DATE: SUN, MAR 17, 1996
Paul,

Just returned from a glamorous all-dyke party. Not just any old all-lesbian party, either. No crew cuts or overalls here. Husband and I were the only boys in a crowd of 30 or so elegant lipstick lesbians of all ethnicities, ranging in age from 25 to 45. Held in an elegant Marin

hilltop home, million-dollar view of hills, bay, oaks, clouds. Lots of
beautiful and intelligent women. Felt proud to be a Bay Area homo,
where the pool of queers is large enough to engender such a sparkling
gathering. Fun to be the token guys too, and George and I both did our
best not to interrupt all the time or hold forth, as is the wont of our
sex. Nice to be enveloped in cream and gray walls, artfully placed
lights. Nice to eat and drink the best. We live in a gilded age. Obvious
clichéd parallels to fourth century Rome, Paris 1788, or Europe 1912. We
fiddle each other as Rome burns, and after us the deluge.

My day was achingly wholesome. Joined my gorgeous buddy Scotty—
buzzed head, studly figure—on a jaunt to Café Flore, outdoor café and
world-navel. The point of the excursion was to entertain and show off
his pseudo-niece, the two-year old child of his housemate and best
friend Sharon. Tatiana is his charge for a good ten days. Scotty wore
an old Queer Nation T-shirt, shades, and dog collar to make clear that
this was no traditional daddy. I teased him that he wanted another
candid photo of himself in the gay press. Beautiful hot day, thus all
the muscles were out. Hundreds of nice-looking guys, a good two dozen
irresistible ones. Though maybe too perfect. Hot house flowers. Biceps
all bought at the same gym, haircuts and tattoos from same bou-
tiques. Still, for all the silliness of passing fashion, beauty commands.

Thanks for your letters of yesterday and today. I wear dumb Calvin-
type shorts, whatever's cheap. Boxers sometimes, like the freedom and
brush of cloth, but then my balls begin to droop to my knees. I had my
own collection of Sears catalogue underwear ads as a lad, which I
burned in my one and only Catholic Reformation at age 12. Hope you're
catching up on your sleep, and that your studies go well. I love the fact
that you're an occasional nekkid housecleaner. Sweet of you too to

indulge the unprepossessing old guy. In the end, how much does it cost one to be sexually kind to the old and homely? Yet it can be very hard to do. Would you want to be a masseur? Money could be quite good. Can be real work though. Advertising, scheduling and pounding people for hours at a time. But you are good enough to eat, and might profit.

Funny isn't it that one always thinks of infatuation in terms of wanting to drink only from the beloved's lips. In my infatuation for you, though, I hope you are enjoying all manner of men. I seek to honor you with depravities of my own. On the other hand, I miss you and think of you all the time, and wish I could taste now the kisses of your mouth. I've never been swept up this way. I look at this short paragraph and think I should delete it. Forgive me for getting carried away. My dick and heart both swell when I think of you.

I wish I had a time machine, to travel back to one of your baby-sitting gigs. Posing as a suburban dad, I'd barge in on you while you had one of my jockeys stuffed in your mouth. Would take you over my knee--your pants are already down around your ankles--and whale away on your delicate little butt until it glowed. Unlike any other spanking you'd ever had, this beating slows down till my hand is caressing your cheeks, wedging itself into your crack with each blow, stroking your puckered little hole with its first hairs. By now you've felt the big boner in my pants, and it isn't long before my dick is out and shoved up your throat. 25 savage strokes and I'm coming in your mouth, till jiz runs out of your nose.

Exhausted, I'm off to bed.

Kevin

FROM KEVIN
DATE: SUNDAY NIGHT, ST. PAT'S

Paul,

Hope your afternoon went well. I don't have anything amusing to
relate. Just restless, thinking about you. Another party this afternoon, a true Bernal Heights fete. About one third queer couples, lots
of little kids. Music from a pair of brilliant pros. Hot sunny day,
another all's-right-with-the-world atmosphere. Too healthy for me:
the bubbly was Martinelli's, the coffee was decaf, the bagels lacked
lox, much less little piggy sausages. There was no groping of
strangers behind doors. Serious chocolate though, and don't mean to
complain: the people were friendly and smart.

Maybe I'll call you. I cast my attention around my messy office.
Unsatisfied with work, with not being paid, with houseguests for
whom I'll have to clean house and act as cicerone. And then I think
of you, and can enjoy good thoughts, full of caffeine, meat, booze
and other substances.

Love,

Kevin

--- ▸ ---

FROM PAUL
DATE: SUN, MAR 17, 1996

Kevin

Thought I'd send some St. Patrick's Day greetings your way. My
bathrobe has green stripes interwoven into the plaid, so I'm feeling
a little Patrick-like.

Thanks for the underwear info--but when is your birthday? Like a teenager I'm dying to know so I can find out what your sign is and then I can go look at stupid astrology books to see if we're compatible. Now I feel like deleting what I've just written, but I'll be brave and just send it along. I too feel as though I've never felt this way before--I've had my crushes, but they were always on people who ultimately turned out to be uninteresting or disappointing in some way. The reverse seems to be the case with you.

I had a nice night's sleep last night--ten hours of it, actually. So I'm going to get showered and dressed and do some studying before I head over to Samuel's. His lover is away, and I think he's a little lonely, so he's having a group of students to his house for brunch.

Have a good day, and I'll check in on you later tonight.
Showering you with shamrocks,

Paul

--- ▶ ---

FROM KEVIN
DATE: MONDAY, MARCH 18, 4:00 P.M.
Paul,

Finally got a dick in my mouth. Little perv named Nate, with whom I've been exchanging messages. Just finished our first session, should be more, he wants a regular outlet. Had jacked off twice before finally connecting with me and coming over. 25 years old, 5'8", 140 lbs, very smooth skin, Italian or assimilated Hispanic. Glossy black hair, shades, cute rather than handsome. Enthusiastic, though. Friendly and businesslike about being sucked off. Pressed for time, so told me to suck fast and deep, with my hand tight under his balls. Pretty dick, but not large. Nice big testicles. Came down my throat, as previously agreed.

7:00 p.m.: A few hours later, connect with a certain Lee. Hop on my bike to his humble motel-suite apartment. Mid-thirties, good features but a slightly wrecked aspect. His body turns out to be pale and smooth, and a tad flabby in the gut. But I don't mind. In fact, his nervousness and reticence are a real turn on. How long have you been doing this, he asks. Oh, since about age 13. Later: How can you do that? Only one girl was ever able to do that for me, get it all the way down. Well, I say, I was 69ing with a buddy in high school and all of a sudden his dick went all the way down, the gag reflex was gone. Then: What would you say my dick is like? Not from vanity, just want to hear what you think. Hmm. Bigger than average, nicely shaped, darker cock and balls than surrounding skin, also nice small dark bush.

He's on the verge of cumming the whole time. Tells me to slow down. Pulls away again and again, wants it to last. Dick stays upright, rock hard. I enjoy going slow, licking his balls, sliding tongue up the shaft, concentrating on the head. Says he wants to feel my dick. My pants are off, and I'm hard. He squeezes it like someone judging an unfamiliar object. After 15 minutes of slow work and holding off, he says he won't be able to hold back much longer. He warns me when he's near, and I only pump harder, letting him spurt deep down my throat. He pulls up his pants pretty quickly. Second thoughts? Shakes hands with sincere sounding but sheepish thanks. Says he'll probably be in touch. I ride home with the taste of cum lingering at the back of my throat, crotch sweat on my fingers.

1:00 p.m.: Thinking of our conversation last night. Remembering my first impression of you at the baths. Me craning up from the cocksuckers' pit, you pausing and moving away. My assumption that you were shy, uninterested in public debauchery, on the lookout for someone as young and handsome as yourself. Someone to have vanilla sex with in a private room. How lucky I felt then to find myself, later, in a cubicle with you.

Thinking also about my early cocksucking days. Those first sexual experiences were all in a suburban Montgomery Ward toilet. The stalls were covered with sexy graffiti and obscene drawings. I think it was the drawings that grabbed me first. My private Lascaux caves. Crude drawings of boys with their cartoon members dripping, pointed at each other's mouths. I thought, are we supposed to pee in each other's mouths? I was looking for pointers, amazed at how arresting the images were.

I wonder if I can sort out these distant events. The older man who invited me into his stall, stroked my 11 year-old body and sucked my dick, saying again and again: so young, so dangerous. The older man (the same one?) who sucked my dick and then coaxed me into holding his, then kissing the top of the shaft, then kissing the head, then: go ahead, take the tip in your mouth. Sucked his glans for two seconds. Spat and spat afterwards, looking for my family in the mall. Unable to shake the taste. Certain I was stained, corrupted. A little Lady Macbeth washing her hands. The teenager, slender muscular body, curly black bush, jacking himself and smiling at me through the glory hole--before I knew what jacking off was. The older guy who slipped me a note--not a phone number, something else, an invitation to sex--scribbled on a carefully torn patch of nude magazine photo. I kept it a long time, a miniature talisman of sex, a porn shot of a heavy-testicled youth, the most beautiful thing I had ever seen. The pair of hands that reached under the stall wall to finger

my butthole and pump my dick, my first sustained jacking. I didn't
fully get the point of this, understand the importance of repetition,
the idea that something was building. Until, that is, sensations began
to build. With a sense of panic, felt something rising in my crotch.
Thought it must be a weird impulse to piss. Pulled away from his
hands in time to spray my first ejaculation on the toilet seat. Felt
like something had been pulled almost painfully, from deep within
me. Was shaky afterwards. Leaned down (a different time?) to see a
huge dick spout white gouts over a man's hand.

But when did I fixate on swallowing cum? I don't think anyone
took my load on those early occasions. I think I remembered the
cave paintings, and ate my own cum off my hands. Trained myself to
suck my own cock, and could get half of it in for a few jabs at a
time. Often, often came on my face and into my open mouth. Always
loved it, though I can't say that objectively it tastes good.

As I told you last night, I vividly remember eating Sean's sperm.
Among my friends at my new high school was slender long-haired
Sean: blond, angelic, cerebral, studiously mellow. He resisted my
advances until surprising me one night by kissing me violently,
crushing lips against teeth, pushing tongues deep. That first time I
was soon sucking his dick in the front seat of a car in a wooded
suburban October street. He came quickly, and I greedily wanted it
all. This surprised him more than anything else.

Eating cum is sympathetic magic, incorporating the essence of
the other. Taking in his maleness. It is a supreme act of affection
and tenderness: yes I will take this from you, I want you to expel
that which is of you into me. It's the Eucharist.

Loved hearing your voice. Hope your 18th has gone well. I think of your eventual return north, of the orgies I will program for you. Only the best, and the sleaziest, for my beautiful friend Paul.

Kevin

--- ▶ ---

FROM PAUL

DATE: MON, MAR 18

Kevin

I woke up not long ago recalling a series of vaguely erotic dreams about beautiful men. I know that they were all versions of you.

It was so great to hear your voice again--you have a terribly sexy voice, and it was all I could do to keep from getting you to talk dirty to me. My cock was certainly stiff more than once during the conversation as it was. Strange how similar and yet how different our 13-year-old precocious sexual selves acted. I could never have answered an ad like you, but I could certainly detect cruising places in urban settings pretty adeptly. Only fooled around with one "friend," and he was hardly a friend. He was younger than me, a bully who lived near my house, and he'd come over after school to "cornhole" me. He hadn't yet developed a mature set of genitali a, but he still felt good pretending to poke his puny prick into my still virgin asshole. He couldn't ejaculate either, so he would jerk me off and be amazed at what a pubescent cock could produce.

It sounds as though you'll have your hands full of houseguests this month. I hope it doesn't get you frustrated. Of course, if playing the host keeps you from the Campus Theater or the Steamworks for too long, you'll be even that much more hyped for a sucking spree when visitors are gone. I've never been to the Campus Theater, and

>d.o.c.

I'd love for you to show me the ropes, as it were, to cocksucking
around San Francisco Bay. Once again, I think we make a pretty good
team of shameless cum-slurping bottom boys. Missionary companions, if you will.

So now I'm off to run some errands, and then I promised myself I
would begin writing today, so I'll see if anything comes up before
then, but I'm afraid I won't be able to dedicate much time to searching out loads. Damn.

Wishing I'd had my arms around you last night,
Paul

--- ▶ ---

FROM: PAUL
DATE: WEDS, MAR 20
Kevin,
I got five whole pages of this paper written, and my roommate
(who's done with all his papers, damn him) was sweet enough to
bring a bottle home, so I've been sipping (between gulps) whiskey
for the last couple of hours and I'm feeling kinda drunk now. It's
nice though. Haven't done whiskey for a while.

So I went up to Blue Cat Canyon again this afternoon. I was really
horny and really wanting to find more inventive ways of procrasti-
nating. I get there and immediately I run into a married man (ring on
the left hand) who seems real skittish. He lets me suck him, but he
keeps ducking behind bushes whenever he thinks someone is
approaching. I suck him to completion and he smiles, says "I've
never cum in someone's mouth before." I believe him, of course.

Next I work on a Latino boy who's been sitting in his Trans-Am with his sweatpants around his thighs stroking his cock. Lots of small talk, he wants to head down by the creek, so we go, and I suck him, he sucks me, we get into weird positions--not so comfortable when you're on rocks and shrubbery, but he finally cums into my mouth. For some reason it tastes weird, so I spit, and I see blood in the spittle. I look back at his dick, and sure enough he has blood on the tip of his dick. Why is he bleeding when he comes? It grosses me out for a minute, but I get myself together. I'll go home now, I think, but then I see a guy I did some weeks before pull up--he had a great dick and came buckets on my face, so I follow him to a spot near the stream.

He kicks back and lets me suck on his cock while he dishes out some fine verbal abuse. When he's close, he mutters, "Take it cause I don't want it on my pants." Nonetheless he stands up and starts spurting onto my face. His cum is voluminous as well as thick and he gets a good deal in my mouth anyway. Takes off right away.

I wipe it off my face and into my mouth. I decide to leave since it's already after two and I should get going on this damned paper, but I run into a very well-built and stocky Hispanic guy who's wearing a pair of cut-off sweats and swinging like a pendulum inside them. Like a hypnotized subject, I follow him to a spot where he unbuckles my pants, pulls them down and starts stroking my dick. I do the same to him, and he pushes me down to his uncut cock--about 6"--and I go to work on it. He gets rougher with my head--soon he's got a handful of hair and is jerking my head off and onto his cock. Every so often he works on my tits--either with his mouth or his fingers. He's relent-less. My left tit still feels like it's being yanked off. He also gets the idea that I want to be treated like a pig, so he starts to feel my ass and stick his finger into my hole. Why not? So he puts two (!) con-

>d.o.c.

doms onto his dick, turns me around and tries to poke it into my ass without further ado. Well, I need just a wee bit more lube than that pathetic film of nearly nonexistent nonoxynol-9 that condoms come so utterly unequipped with, so I ask him to spit on my ass, at least. He does, and I concentrate on receiving him, and he slides himself into me without much pain. Starts fucking me like a jackhammer, and soon I can feel his momentum reaching a peak. He's gasping and plunging into me even deeper than before, so I know that he's filling those condoms with his cum. Oh, I forgot to mention that we'd entirely stripped out there, so we were both utterly naked through most of this. It was pretty hot, although it would have been hotter had you stumbled across us and had me suck on you while he fucked me.

Went home and napped a bit, and wrote for most of the evening. Now I know I'll get this paper written; it's just a matter of getting started for me. I took a break for dinner and The Simpsons. Lisa is one of my heroes.

So have a good night--I hope your married man was good enough to eat. Missing you as much as ever,

Paul

--- ▶ ---

FROM PAUL
DATE: WEDS, MAR 20
Kevin

I just got back from friends' where we (they'd invited two other guests) ate chicken Kiev and home-made cole slaw. Michael and his friend Mark, a drag queen trying to get a job in Vegas, went off to the hot tub and Matthew sucked me off on the living room couch. I

met him at Fairmount Park last November, and that time he sucked
me on the circular benches in the rose garden before we held one
another against the cold.

My French final was a bitch--I hadn't studied irregular formation for
future simple, so I know I missed a good handful at the end of the test.
I also wanted to get out of the testing room fast because my allergies
were acting up and I needed to blow my nose. So I headed right over to
the P.E. men's room where I was lucky enough to get three loads in
succession. The first was from a middle-aged man with short short red
hair and a beard and mustache. He had a fair-sized cock and a wedding
ring. He was trigger happy, and came soon after I'd begun to suck on
him. He murmured "I'm cumming" as a warning, but I only pushed my
mouth further down on his pulsing cock. He thanked me, smiled and
waved, and left just as a new man came to take his place.

This one I'd done before--a real throwback from the 70s, with
Hawaiian shirt and gold chain to match his feathered hair. But he had
an enormous dick that twisted around and down in the most fascinat-
ing manner. How to get this one down my throat? He was very verbal
in a geeky sort of way, but I ignored his canned porno monologue and
concentrated on how to negotiate the most contorted cock I've ever
run across. He loved having the head worked on, so I didn't HAVE to get
the corkscrew down my gullet, but I wanted to anyway. He left his
stall and came over to mine, I opened the door and fell to my knees. In
this position I could tilt my head to the left and his cock would fit nicely down my throat. However, this was only comfortable for so long.
Now he wants to 69, and I'm not so keen about getting on the cum and
piss-stained floor--as much as I like it for ambience's sake. I'm able
to work out a position in which we can reach one another's cocks

nicely without my having to touch the floor any more than necessary. He's totally turned on by this, and I can feel him getting closer. I take my mouth off his dick and tell him that I want to take his load in my mouth. He looks horrified at first: "You want to swallow it?" h e asks. I nod my head, and his shocked reaction melts into a wicked smile. Seconds later I'm gulping his load as he squirms on the filthy floor.

After I've listened to a swimmer take a genuine dump a few stalls down from me, a new boy occupies the stall next to mine, and I slowly peer through the hacksawed hole that measures about 1' square. To my utter delight I've landed a truly beautiful surfer clone with sandy, longish hair, full parted lips, perfectly tanned from head to toe, and sporting what looks to be a promising piece of meat. I motion for him to place his cock through the hole, and he crouches--must be about 6'2"--to push it through. As I approach his cock with an eager mouth, I notice his mammoth thighs and a healthy bush of fine, black pubic hair. My sucking on his cock only makes it grow, and he immediately begins to fuck my face with plenty of moaning and gasping. I look up at his face peering at me over the stall divider and he has a sexy gap between his front teeth. He pulls away and grabs the base of his cock while fluid starts to ooze from his piss-slit and down his stout shaft. I'm praying that this isn't his orgasm because I want that coating the interior of my mouth. False alarm--and he puts his dripping cock back into my hungry mouth. I suck to the base while pubic hair tickles my nostrils. Not much more sucking is needed and I soon feel his dick twitch and bounce between my lips. I push myself all the way back down on his meat, and, inspired by my cocksucking hero in Berkeley, I clench my throat as he shoots. He seems slightly embarrassed as he pulls up his dark gray paisley briefs that can barely contain his still tumescent organ. I want so badly to give him my phone number and tell him that anytime he needs a release he can call me, but I can't muster up enough courage.

Meanwhile, the crookedest dick in the world is back, and I'm only lukewarm about sucking him again. But he comes to my stall door with a resilient hard-on, so I'm back on my knees working his corkscrew-cock down my throat again. Soon he has stepped out of his pants and briefs and has begun to unbutton his shirt. This is going a bit further than I want, so I start shooting my load on the floor, giving me a proper excuse to get the hell out of there.

Thus was my afternoon--and it really only took about an hour and a half. I treat myself to a chile verde burrito for lunch and head home to read a few more academic articles.

I was tempted to call you tonight so I could once again hear the voice that makes my heart skip and my cock throb, but I'm afraid I'll just blather about nothing again--stunned stupid that such a sexy, brilliant man would even give me the time of day. You have me in the palm of your cum-coated hand.

Sleep well,
Paul

--- ▶ ---

FROM KEVIN
DATE: WEDNESDAY, MARCH 20
Paul,
Worried about my mental health. Just spent most of the day and night at the Campus Theater, again. Not that it was even that amus-

ing, in terms of numbers or quality of available men and boys. No,
something obsessional here. Anyway, had a few errands in town, so
used that as an excuse....

As sometimes happens, scored best at the beginning. Pegged a
handsome barrel-chested, dark-haired early 30s businessman as
available, drew him into a quiet corner to suck his fat dick. Sensed
he was bi, closeted, or novice--or some combination. Startled by an
announcement of the next show, he asked if what we were doing was
cool. I answered that we would only be disturbed, if at all, by guys
who wanted to join in. He relaxed, let me deepthroat him, jacked my
hard dick, and wanted to cum quickly. Didn't expect me to take his
load, I didn't insist.

Joel, a perfectly beautiful go go boy, was next course. As he
worked the sparse crowd in the dingy, intimate little arena, I was
delighted to see that he permitted a nice-looking homo to suck his
dick, protected as they were by the shadows. So when he got to me I
was emboldened to swallow his long erection and massage it with my
throat muscles, in a much more exposed position. He seemed to
enjoy it as much as I. Felt such gratitude to him for his grace, for
his indulgence, for his generosity in letting me finger his hole and
suck his nipples and dick. As he moved on I scooted over to the guy
who had sucked him first, exchanged a few words. Agreed that if he
came by again we'd suck him together.

He didn't. Retired instead to his private prostitution sessions. I
went off with aforementioned cocksucker. We worked on each other,
warm affectionate standup sex. Unremarkable physically, but perfectly tasty for the moment. He too shot into the air, without too
many regrets on my part.

I lounged then in equally dreary parlor adjacent to "shower room", the sex-for-pay venue. Struck up conversation with go go boy from earlier, Joel, who turned out to be a much-employed actor, affable, even enthusiastic about posing for my photography group. When we parted, I stood to embrace him. He was still naked. In his ear, I thanked him for letting me suck him in full view of the crowd. He graciously demurred, then said: I think of this place as church. I know some of the other guys don't, but I think of this as holy. You know: This is my body....

We exchanged cards. I went off to class. Thought how much I'd rather be photographing you than our perfectly presentable model, Anthony. How I'd like to shoot you in dignified academic poses, and in others with a cock deep in your mouth and up your ass. Incorrigible, I left early to return to the Campus. Porn star Alec Powers (typical dopey stage name) would repeat the 5:30 show that I'd barely caught with another at 9:30. I've seen plenty of cute porn stars. But this body, face and smile were so compelling that I wanted to see him again. Muscular but slender body, rich in golden curves, but not steroid-overdone like so many. A genuine smile, enjoying the miracle of his own deliciousness, and getting off on the adoration of the crowd. Generous with his body, too. To a point. Happy to let me run my hands everywhere, over extraordinarily pretty convex mounds of ass and pecs. Happy enough about my mouth on his stomach and my fingers in the blond hairs of his asshole. But wouldn't let me suck him, even when I moved to the deepest shadows and begged. Prerogatives of stardom.

In the absence of studly guys, I let some others suck me, even getting into two different threeway scenes: a boyish little Asian guy worked me and a bespectacled, jolly 40-year-old married guy. Sucked both cocks in turn, offered his ass to each of us for faux-fucking, as we rubbed and pushed. Also facefucked a handsome head in the darkness, then joined by same married man. Finally, played with the last performer of the evening, a skinny black kid with a monster dick. He let me lick the head, fleetingly, and got very passionate with me, even taking my hard-on--just briefly--in his mouth.

Paul, maybe I've gone over the edge. Tomorrow I'll work, be responsible. I haven't cum yet, and will masturbate thinking about new ways to give you pleasure.

Only just now read both your messages. They are so sexy that my mind spins. Surfers and brutal Mexicans. I am overcome with affection and admiration for you. My cock aches for you. I want to exchange kisses again with your beautiful mouth, filled again with a stranger's cum.

Godspeed,

Kevin

--- ▶ ---

FROM PAUL
DATE: THURS, MAR 21
Kevin,

Very uneventful day--got more writing done and I'm liking this project more and more as I think about what I could do with the time and research I'd need.

I was ecstatic to receive the photos of you--both turned me on to no end. Who in the hell was that stud with such enormous forearms and massive hands? You look terrific sucking on his cock--and you look as cute as I'd remembered with your visor and a half-embarrassed smile. Can't stop thinking of you either.

My friend Robert called this morning and asked me if I wanted to ride up to SF with him the weekend of the 30th, but a good friend of mine is visiting on the 31st (checking out UCLA) and I know you have lots of company. God, I want to see you so badly.

Also, my roommate and I went downtown (yes, there is a downtown here) and stopped in at a local bookstore where I was thrilled to see a stack of your books. So many things remind me of you, make me remember our only day together, and I so long to have you near me more often. I have a friend (just a friend, and he's very very straight) over, so I have to cut this short. Good thing too or I'd just blubber on about how much I love you.

More tomorrow--hope your first day of Spring was memorable,
Paul

 --- ---

FROM PAUL
DATE: FRI, MAR 22
Kevin,
Thank God I'm nearly done with this damn paper. I'm happy with it on one level--I'm beginning to explore Orientalism in relation to homosexuality in the eighteenth century in interesting (to me) ways, but I'm also finding I have to do so much biographical and historical background--not to mention plot summaries--because the prof. I'm writing this for is not very familiar with any aspect of what I'm writing about. To top it all off, a friend of mine (the one who failed to set me up with his friends in SF that night I ended up at the baths--and

I'm still very happy those plans didn't materialize) came over and read what I'd written so far. He had some really confused and fairly negative comments about what I'd done, and this, of course, left me riddled with self-doubt and despondency. Well, fuck it--I'm going to polish it off tomorrow and turn it in regardless. I need to get on with my spring break!

Today I had to run to the library and look up a few of my sources, so hoping to recap my success at the massive glory hole in the old P.E. building, I decided to make an appearance there. Moments after I'd sat my bare ass on the porcelain seat, a man (a librarian? a professor?) I've sucked a number of times came in and perched himself. He has a huge dick that never seems to get fully stiff, and I normally enjoy having him spurt his load all over my face. I DO enjoy a face sprayed with cum. He looks to be in his mid-forties with hip, shorn head, gray Levi's and a blazer. He wears white Calvin Klein briefs that are always impeccably clean. I hadn't been sucking him for long when a person came into the restroom and sat in the stall a couple down from mine.

We wait to see if the newcomer is going to start grunting or if he's going to start peering at us from beneath his stall divider. He chooses the latter, and to my delight I recognize surfer-clone from the other day. He's shy, however, and though he's content to peer at anything we might be doing from under his stall, he won't come any closer even when I motion for him to do so. So I suck on the prof. hoping to get him off and get to the surfer before the boy loses patience. The prof. cums in my mouth, and then leaves, so I wait for the boy to come and take his spot on the other side of the glory hole.

He's beautiful in a very unreal Southern California beer-ad kind of way--I suck on him for a few moments, but soon another visitor comes into the restroom and occupies the empty stall just on the other side of me. This guy wastes no time, and immediately stands up, looks over the short divider, and I can tell he's jacking himself off too. He's black and athletic--probably drops into the men's room after a workout or a basketball game to get his testosterone-tormented nuts off before heading home. I tell him to come into my stall thinking the surfer boy will want to watch me give this guy head. This black jock has a smallish dick, but likes to be verbal-every time I take my mouth off his cock he mutters, "ho, keep sucking it" as if to reassure me that it will pay off eventually. In a very short time, he's making I'm-cumming noises, so I swallow the whole of his dick and feel his load squirting against the back of my throat.

He leaves right away, and I'm back on the hornier-than-ever surfer whose cock is ready to burst. He cums quickly and copiously into my swallowing mouth, sits back on the toilet, but doesn't leave. I quickly tear a strip of paper on which I pen my name and phone number. I hand it to him through the hole and say to call me when he feels like it. He's still hard and jerking his cock. "Can you cum again?" I ask, knowing full well that this very young, very horny stud could be cumming four or five times a day. He nods his head, and so I motion for him to put his hard dick back through the hole. I suck on him for a couple of minutes, but some noisy conversationalists come into the urinal area and break the spell. Surfer boy pulls his pants back up and starts to leave. I stand up to look at him--to beg him with my eyes to give me another shot of boy-cum--but he mouths "I've got a final."

Three's a charm, so I leave too to find some lunch: salmon spring

rolls. As I'm paying for them, surfer boy appears opposite me at the
register with his Pizza Hut personal pizza and breadsticks. I act cool--
don't look at him because he's nervous and would never want anyone to expect that this grad student buying a geeky sushi plate has
just sucked the juice out of his uncontrollable cock less than twenty
minutes before. I pass him sitting on a bench and eating his pizza,
and choose a place out of his line of vision to eat my lunch. I somehow hope that this behavior will only incite him to call me soon.

I hope your day was productive--in whatever way that may be--
and that none of YOUR so-called friends critiqued your work in ruth-
less and unhelpful ways. I'll be thinking of you as I go to sleep
tonight. In fact, I know I'll be releasing a load while gazing at the
amazing photo of you sucking a far-too-beautiful man to completion, and I'll be imagining you bringing that cum-filled mouth to
mine and placing a load of jism onto my tongue that we'll savor
together in a kissing frenzy. My dick is rock hard now just thinking
about it. Have I ever yearned for someone's company like this
before? I know I haven't.

Your companion in cocksucking,

Paul

--- ▶ ---

FROM KEVIN
DATE: FRIDAY, MARCH 22

Paul

A brief note to thank you for your latest. So hot! So glad that you got
another load from the surfer, much less from the black guy and the
librarian! Triumph! Just getting the phone number in the guy's hand

is satisfying, knowing that it is burning a hole in his pocket on his walk home. He'll have to think that getting his cock sucked isn't nec-essarily only a matter of tearoom serendipity, but that there is a very handsome, very proficient cum-thirsty young man just a phone call away.... I hope he acts on it. I like the idea of a steady routing, of being on call to a couple of guys. Has happened a few times for me, and I want more. Hate to think that guys as spunky as your blond boy are hand-jobbing it when they could be feeding you.

Much love,

Kevin

--- ▶ ---

FROM: KEVIN

DATE: SPRING EQUINOX

Paul,

I lied. Told you I would knuckle down to work, but had an errand in downtown Oakland, so found myself stopping at that pearl of culture, Hollywood Books. An emporium of sleaze, it boasts video token booths. Rented a yummy Falcon video (Siberian Somethings: Boys, Butts, Huskies?), very young pretty Russian boys with huge dicks, lots of kissing, plenty of real erections throughout. Refreshing after the steroids and crank-filled overly-pneumatic dudes of so much LA porn. Let several guys suck my dick through the glory hole: an old codger, a middle aged black dad, a younger black guy, a sexy South American in glasses, whom I invited into my lair. Nice brown body, nice round butt, nice heavy balls and dick down my throat, but suddenly less avid about me and more interested in whoever was in the next booth. Finally kicked him out. An Israeli masturbated him-

self to climax with my dick in his mouth, a big Samoan sucked me
until I pulled out and jacked myself until cumming. But the best,
and most frustrating, moment of the day came near the beginning. A
truly studly boy, early 20s, perfect features, bright eyes and kiss-
able lips, regulation baseball cap and long shorts, declined my fixed
stare as I set up my movie rental. He was far and away the prettiest
guy of the day, but I resigned myself to missing out. Then, to my
surprise, I realized that he was in the next booth eyeing me
through the glory hole. He wanted to see my dick as much as I wanted to see his! Finally, he stuck his big thing through the hole: 3 or
4" across, his cock barely fit through the hole, and it was as long
as it was thick. I take back what I said yesterday about cum not
tasting good. His pre-cum was delicious, and I got a few fresh drops
with each stroke. I was frustrated by the wall. Glory holes are well
and good when you don't care much about the guy on the other side,
but I wanted to get all of him down, wanted his balls banging against
my chin. He pulled out and wanted to suck me, so I complied. After a
bit I withdrew, wanting to join him on the other side of the wall. But
I looked over just in time to see him spill his seed uselessly and
button himself up to leave. Damn. I waved my tongue through the
hole, wanting his jism. Waved a note through the hole, reading:
Kevin--cocksucker--call anytime. But all to no avail. He was satisfied with eight minutes of anonymous dick. I wanted more: to eat his
load, preferably more than once. I should be happy that I got what I
did, but it is always thus, yes? If he ignores me, I wish I had somehow engaged him. If I have some sex with him, I wish I had had
more. If I have him once, I want him two or three more times. The
dynamic of sexual craving is a paradoxical desire to have someone

the three or four times (or 20 or 40) it takes to satisfy one's
curiosity, to feel that one has truly had him.

Did get some work done, finally. And exchanged phone calls with
several tricks, who are piling themselves up for tomorrow afternoon. We'll see. And no more of this self-deprecating stuff. You are
in no way my inferior in anything, and it is I who have ten years of
hard wear and tear on you. Smart and handsome and depraved,
you're an angel of sex. I want to eat crème fraiche off your cock,
want to tongue champagne from your asshole. I want to rob a bank
or mug Republicans and spend fortunes on you. I want to lead you
through the gutters of Paris and Berlin on a diamond leash, letting
only the most testosterone-poisoned pay homage to you with their
oceans of semen. I think of you all the time. How many times have I
written those words already, how many more thought them?

The boy who humped you as a lad never achieved real penetra-
tion? How did you lose your cherry? My cock stands at attention as I
think about the deflowering of young Paul. I don't let myself get
fucked very often. It remains a huge mental turn on for me, but
often too intense to do. Recovery, too, is always an issue. I limp
around for a day afterward. Nothing so amazing, though, as being
completely subjugated by a hard-dicked fucker, being impaled on a
lance that stabs and stabs. Theresa of Avila knew wherefrom she
spake, pierced again and again by the huge flaming spear of divine
love, wielded by a boy-angel with an executioner's smile.

With love for my executioner,

Kevin

--- ▶ ---

FROM: KEVIN

DATE: FRIDAY, MARCH 22, 12:30 A.M.

Paul,

Glad you got the photos. I'm not much to look at, but Don and his big dick in my face are nice. Nice too that you found a pile of my books at the bookshop. It is an odd, pleasant feeling to hear that they've been seen here or there, in places I've never been. Or places where I've just arrived. Feels like I've arrived before I've arrived.

Not much news. My many tricks failed to follow through, not so surprisingly: half Italian–half Japanese James, a little too wholesome in his banker's drag when I met him the other day for coffee and mutual audition; 30-year-old virgin Rusty, a Sacramento crypto-homo, aching to have sex with a feller, his hard dick pearlying up with pre-cum when he posed for my camera, but unable as of yet to take the plunge; Jason the bisexual grad student, whose cum I had the pleasure of drinking last week. All were supposed to get in touch but didn't. This doesn't count the black married plumber, and a few more guys whose voices I haven't heard yet, whom I know so far only by their online exclamation marks. Notably, there's one guy, hand-some (he says) Sicilian-American 38 year old who hasn't messed around with a guy since he was 13 (he says), and wants to do so now, with me. If I suck him well, he hopes to get his wife in on it. He's been trying to work her up to a three-way. Asks if it's OK if he jacks me off, says I might have to experience his throat too. I'll believe it when I feel it. Fun to coax the process along, in any event. Even if he chickens out, or turns out to be a clown: another chink opened in the armor of American manhood, more proof--however anecdotal--that everybody loves dick.

Now Kenneth did come through, and I happily sucked him off for the third time. For the first time he sucked me. My hard-on was bobbing in easy reach, he couldn't stop himself from gobbling me down with some violence. I like our jokey friendly manner with each other. Those feet though. Whew. He's always quite clean, but his shoes must be old because I kept getting intermittent whiffs of Gorgonzola from down south.

Got a lot of work done, cycled round town on this beautiful spring day, enjoyed having a little money in my pocket, saw a little Canadian film tonight called Love and Human Remains on tape, worthwhile in many respects, silly in others. So withal a good day. Hope your allergies don't trouble you too much. Suddenly driven to call you, but it's too late, and I know most of what I want to say can't be said in words anyway. Just want to stroke your face, ruffle your hair, and caress your long back and beautiful ass. Someday soon. Half a mind to get a car somehow and drive down. Have an errand that could justify it. You wouldn't have to put me up. I'd be happy just to hide my face for a while against your sweet skin.

Kevin

--- ▶ ---

FROM: KEVIN
DATE: FRIDAY, MARCH 22, ALMOST MIDNIGHT
Dear Paul,

Just off the phone with a guy named Michael, 27 years old, German-Swiss-Italian, tall and slim, 9" dick. Protracted phone sex, but look-ing forward to tomorrow night when, by arrangement, I go to his place on Russian Hill to suck the real thing. He's as enthusiastic as I am about my taking his load, hope it works out.

Spent the evening à quatre with two old friends who've recently become an item. She's one of my oldest friends, he is one of George's. Lovely dinner, great wine and conversation. Went out into his rural garden afterward to pick out the comet, a fuzzy sentinel in the northern sky. All night I thought about how I wanted to confide in my slender, chic buddy Elisa that I had this extraordinary e-mail romance, that there was this beautiful boy I had to tell her about, that his lewdness, coupled with mine, inspired the most restless feelings of lust, warmth and regard in my heart, brain and dick. But of course I didn't.

I loved hearing your voice again today. Wanted to say so much, but heard myself sounding officious and businesslike instead. I entertain thoughts of desperate acts. I want to give you things, pamper you, show you the beautiful and lewd pleasures of Europe, for example. Want to procure for you huge Brazilian cocks, Australian top men, Hungarian boy-whores.

For the moment I have nothing for you but words on a computer screen and my passionate regard.

Kevin

--- ▶ ---

FROM: PAUL
DATE: SAT, MAR 23
Kevin,
Finished my papers, and started drinking too early. I'm just zonked. Went to my friend's place to watch X-Files and then we saw Almodovar's Matador. It was wonderful to hear your voice again

today. I feel just awkward enough talking to you over the phone so
that I can hardly get beyond mundane topics like how to print out
copies of my e-mail. I'd really love to say so much more, but I get
self-conscious. In any case, I'd love to have you stay with me on
your way to San Diego--in fact, there are a few good baths there we
could terrorize together. Sleep well, and I'll talk to you tomorrow.

I'm off to a party we're throwing for my roommate Jon, and then
we go to Palm Springs. Hope you were successful with your phone
sex partner--one of these days I need to tell you about how I invented phone sex for myself at the age of 13....

If only I could nestle my nose in your nuts tonight....

Paul

--- ⬆ ---

FROM: KEVIN
DATE: SUNDAY, MARCH 24, 8:00 P.M.
Paul,

Miss you. Talking to you in my head all the time. My news: last night,
made the trip to meet Michael, last night's phone sex. Mutually pleased
on meeting. He's young, wears cool little glasses, blond, slender and
almost shockingly boyish. Maybe 27, but must constantly be carded to
prove he's 21. I get the house tour; he's having his spacious 20s flat
redone, obviously a prosperous boy. Then I realize I know him: friend
and business partner of good friends, a real success as designer and
businessman--really a phenomenon. Who's the kid with the brainy dog
and Mr. Wizard?--that's who Michael looks like. But in this boyish
package is a well-adjusted workaholic, a capable young master of his
competitive craft. I don't let on--I don't want any awkwardness about

having friends in common get in the way of our having sex. Astonished at his naked body, childishly slender shoulders, miniature pink nipples, milky skin, and a beautiful fat dick down to his knees.

There follows an hour and a half of hard work and real pleasure. Sucking his dick is much harder to do than with any normal guy's—as well as going deep, I have to keep my mouth open wide, my teeth off him. He's pleased and demanding. Very verbal, he may be youthful even in his voice, but he's no twinkie. Imagine a demanding 16-year-old with a cop's baton between his legs. Big clean balls, smooth muscular thighs, small soft round butt. I suck him in every conceivable position. He bats my face and open mouth with his club, pushes it back into my face. When a big pearl of pre-cum builds up, he makes me slurp it up. He's very appreciative, and rewards me with deep grunts. Asks me if I like his hard dick, if I want his big load. For an hour we're in no hurry, and I work to give his cock a smooth hot hole. With him on his back, me kneeling between his knees, I'm amazed I can get him all the way down.

He moves off the bed, has me kneel below him, while he feeds me his cock. I lie on my back on the bed, my head hanging below the edge, while he stands and deepfucks my throat. I can only manage a few of these strokes at a time before gagging. All night I reproach myself for gagging or altering my rhythm to make my breathing easier; I aspire to being a mechanical cunt. I want him to grab both ears and fuck my head until I pass out, like Ramon Novarro strangled on Valentino's art deco dildo. But when he does I choke especially soon. I haven't gotten there yet, the disembodied hungry mouth. He is forgiving though, and when I move down to tongue his little hole surrounded by a few wet auburn curls, he heaves in deep

pleasure. From my vantage point, my tongue fucking him, I can see
him watching me. I condemn myself for this. No matter how clean
and spicy it is, I shouldn't be eating his butt. I am incredibly turned
on, but I know it's deeply stupid. But his cheeks are so tight and
round, his legs are so pretty spread wide, and his little bud
responds so well to being tongued. For a while he leans over the bed,
his ass in my face, one of his hands pushing his dick back towards
me so I can suck it down to his heavy balls.

He's hard the entire time, and when the moment finally
approaches for his ejaculation, we both work on him with hands and
tongue in turns. He warns me that when he's about to cum he wants
me to take his cock all the way down so he can shoot deep in me.
When he hits shoots, I taste it and move most of the way down. My
mouth keeps filling, but I see I've lost a big drop on his shaft. I
move down to take that, take a breath to swallow everything, then
finally Sun, Mar 17, 1996 to let him, still throbbing, rest in my
throat. Just a few minutes pass before I'm sucking his fat half-hard
dick again. I see the time, ask him if he wants to jack off in my
mouth before I leave. I'm exhausted by now, my jaw aches from
stretching around him, different jaw muscles hurt from stiffening
my tongue in his sphincter asshole. I hope for an easy lie on my
side while he pumps against my lips. No such luck. I'm busy again,
deep-throating him, changing positions, using hands, mouth, tongue.
Again, I fuck his hole with my tongue, watching him watch me. He
sees me pulling my own dripping hard-on, says I have a nice dick.
Asks me if I'd like to fuck his juicy ass with my dick. I muffle a yes
from his wet crack, but I'm taken aback. So, this boytop wants to be
topped. But I suck on, finger his hole while I suck and pump his

dick. This time I want him to come messily over my lips. He tells me to fingerfuck him. His ass clenches around my finger like a clamp, his rectum is soft and hot. That's how he cums, on and in my face.

Afterward I pretend to realize, suddenly, our connection. He isn't displeased really, but is still a little dismayed. He tells me he has never had a real boyfriend. Boys his own age are intimidated, apparently, by his success and traveling schedule. Older guys are attracted to a vanilla cupcake and find instead a busy adult. We exchange assurances that we will repeat soon.

On trek home, plenty of time to think that I was a loser to be 36 in this culture without a car, an asshole to be out all night in the service of servicing another hard cock, an idiot to eat out that pretty ass.

As usual, what happiness or equilibrium I felt, I got from thinking of you. I thought how I would love to slime my tongue up and down Michael's shaft, with you on the other side, how we would wrap tongues at his glans. I thought how I would love to take your load all over my face and open mouth, while he slammed the cum out of you, with his huge cock.

I love you and want to worship your bod, to give you every possible pleasure, to procure for you rare experiences and real riches.
Kevin

--- ▶ ---

FROM: KEVIN
DATE: MONDAY, 1:30A.M.
Paul,
Will be gone til midday Tuesday, then off to SF for evening. Won't be able to communicate until then. Odd to feel cut-off, when we're

already separated by more than 300 miles. Anyway, you should know I will continue to think of you with longing, with hope that you're enjoying yourself.

We're going north to see two good friends, a couple, easterners, smart beautiful guys. Will let you know if anything amusing occurs--certainly not sex. I have an abiding crush on one of them, but we're all married people, it would be too Harold Pinter to do more than flirt. Besides, he is one of nature's innocents, a nineteenth century type, a man in his midthirties, quite handsome, who has had sex with only a handful of people in his life. We are creatures of different species, as much as we admire each other.

Now I must go off and masturbate, imagining, as usual, you, in some constellation of bodies, orifices and cocks.

Kevin

--- ▶ ---

FROM: PAUL
DATE: TUE, MAR 26
Kevin,

I got both your messages--the one about the Russian Hill boy as well as the short note--and I dread your leaving even when I know you're not here with me anyway.

I need to talk to you about something, and I hate doing it over e-mail, but it's been driving me crazy for a while. You kept talking about how nervous you were rimming the 27-year-old prodigy--I imagine that you're justly concerned about hepatitis. In 1991, I tested positive for HIV, although I've remained asymptomatic. Every time you talk about sucking me or what's more taking my cum, I feel so fucking guilty. I want you to know only because I want you to know everything about me. I came so close to telling you both times we talked over the phone, but I keep resisting because everything has been so good with you so far, and I don't want to screw anything up with heavy news.

Ironically, I was always very safe with men before I went to be tested, and I'm still puzzled about being positive with so few "at risk" experiences behind me at 22. About two years ago, I developed a real taste for more exciting sex, and I couldn't see why I shouldn't take cum if I've already got HIV (although I have considered the arguments for why I shouldn't). I consider myself to be quite sage in terms of what others do for/to me; I will let people suck me if they choose to although I've only cum into other people's mouths if I first tell them that I'm positive. I never fuck other people. I don't feel like I'm going to die any time soon, though I won't say I never worry about that either. I want very badly to live a long, long time. There's so much I want to do in this life. I keep telling myself that it's all about narrative--the stories we tell ourselves about our bodies and what they do. We've been telling ourselves some pretty pathetic, even dangerous, stories about AIDS.

I'm telling you this because I love you and feel you love me as well, and I want you to know about me. In fact, I almost feel as though I want you to know more about me than anyone else ever has, but I certainly won't burden you with that now. I only want you to know that I'm thrilled to have you as a confidante and friend, and that I trust you as much as, if not more than, I trust anyone.

I don't expect any condolences from you--in fact, I don't need any because I'm healthy, happy, and here. I just know that if our fantasy correspondence ever plays itself out in the flesh, and if I ever am lucky enough to be in your gilded presence again, I would simply want you to know who and what you are touching.

This is all coming across much more weirdly than I'd hoped--I'm pretty awkward at spilling my guts unless I'm confessing my sexual secrets to you. My stomach is in knots and I feel on the verge of tears. I so wish you were here and that I could hold your hand for just a few minutes. Deep breaths--I'm fine.

My roommate went off to Palm Springs to see his beau. I began my latest tome today and got through the first 100 pages--I've only got 14 more days like that. There's some terrific stuff going on in these letters--lots of "glowing" and "throbbing," and hysteria   is always bubbling just beneath the surface of the text. Nothing more exciting than that happened today. Met a friend for coffee this after-noon and checked out some CDs from the local library: Elgar and Orff. Oscar party at a friend's. I'm half tempted to head to the park tonight and do a bit of cruising, but part of me thinks it will just be too much work. Phone sex? Just beating off? More reading? I'll give it some thought and let you know tomorrow which option I selected.

I hope you and George have had a good time with your beautiful couple and that I hear from you soon after you return, but I'll be patient. I could wait for you for a very long time. To kiss your lips around a fine, swollen cock head would please me to no end right now, but I'm content to have you in my photos, my collection of lewd letters and in my memories.

With ever-increasing regard and affection,

Paul

--- ▶ ---

>d.o.c.

FROM: KEVIN
DATE: TUESDAY, MARCH 26, LATE
Paul

My beautiful boy, I'm ashamed and dismayed that I've subjected you
to such anguish. I'm HIV-positive myself, and have been too stupid to
broach the subject. What was I thinking: that we could assume we
were both positive, without ever speaking of it? Apparently. Kept
intending to bring it up myself but didn't want to break the porn-
spell of our indestructibility: always ready for sex, never tired,
never damaged by too-rough treatment or sexually transmitted
bugs. That is how, in part, I have thought of us, though with another
part of my brain I've assumed you were positive like me, and have
worried that you should be living with such a shadow.

But I broke that spell already with my uneasiness about eating
the ass of little Michael, and sent you into real worry. I am very
very sorry that all the burden of wrestling with this has fallen on
you. I wish I could caress and stroke you now, show you somehow
how much I revere you. I stare at this screen thinking what an idiot
I've been, and hoping to find a way to make it up to you. Yes, it's
hepatitis I worried about, but also parasites and who knows what
else. Psychologically there is something there too. In my foolish
soul, I've decided that cum is clean, and that assholes--especially
on pretty boys with bubble butts--aren't. I worry that I am sliding
deeper into absurd rationalizations.

Whether I am or not, I didn't lose much time in seeing Michael
again, tonight. Made love to his dick almost as avidly as last time,
but really the thing is enormous and exhausting. He is, as you said
of one of yours, high maintenance, and I don't know how much I'll

want to maintain in future. He takes a long time to come, and makes me work. All things I like, usually! Certainly liked eating his little hole again, which really turned both of us on, for all of my hand wringing. Amazing to have my tongue deep in his ass while looking into his eyes. Finally he did come, jacking off into my mouth while his ass clenched around my finger.

The trip went very well. Beautiful scenery, weather, spectacular comet watching. Continued my deep flirtation with Bernd, but still wouldn't consummate it. Though I would like to show him what a really good blowjob is like, in case that fool husband of his hasn't been executing properly his conjugal duties.

Most of all, and always, I think about how I want to give you pleasure, in all ways. I want to coddle you, spoil you, fuck your brains out, have you fucked by the most beautiful men of your choosing. Want to lie with you, sink into your kisses and never come up for air.

I'm wrecked, exhausted; not sure I'm making sense. I'll only repeat myself like a moron if I say what's in my heart: that I love you. I love you. I love you.

Kevin

--- ▶ ---

FROM: PAUL
DATE: TUES, MAR 26
Kevin,
I kept checking my e-mail hoping you'd gotten home, read my message and had a chance to respond to my hysterical outburst. Finally I was too tired to keep it up, so I went to bed just before midnight. I can't tell you how relieved I was to get your post this morning, and have you reas-

sure me with all the eloquence and tenderness with which you've always written to me. Kevin, you are the most singular fellow! I love you more than ever. If only you had been next to me as I awoke this morning--I would have kissed your sleeping, half-parted lips and then removed my oral caresses to your morning hard-on to take in your day's first load. And then I would have made you breakfast!

Monday night I did head out to the park, but I was distraught. I don't know why I got myself so wound up on Monday. I didn't even get through the park before I parked, walked toward the starlit lake at the park's center, and basically accosted the first male that walked near me. He was a very short, very fuzzy and very chubby man with his fly unzipped and his cock already hard. We debated a bit about who would suck whom. I let him suck me a bit, but then told him I was out here to suck cock and take cum. He resigned himself to this idea, and I began to suck him furiously. For all his gasping and heaving I couldn't get him to shoot. Soon we had a visitor watching us, so I turned to the new dick and sucked on it for a while. Soon the little fellow was bearing down to shoot so I leapt onto his pulsing cock, but was only able to take the first couple of squirts because the visitor told us there were cops coming. I stand and look wildly about me, but there are no cops. Foiled.

I go to a bench near the lake thinking that I shouldn't have come and that tonight I'm less searching for pleasure than I am for self-destruction. The chubby man finds me again, and starts kissing my mouth. He wants to take me home and fuck me. I resist, but he seems to ache for it, so I consent. We get to his apartment--a filthy parody of a bachelor pad--and begin to 69 on his bed. I lie and tell him that I've got guests I've left at home so I need to get going. He puts a condom on, and I slide onto his spitcoated, sheathed cock very easily, because it's so small. I talk dirty, wriggle, change positions--anything to get him off so I can go find what I was really out for: more cum. He moans and squirms, but never explodes. He insists on watching me shoot first. I resist, but I look around me--at the cigarette butts on the floor, the shit-stained underwear spilling out of the closet, the condom wrappers on the dresser--and decide to cum and get this night over with.

He gives me his number and tells me all about his job with the city's utility company. I thank him and get the hell out of hell out of there. I bypass the park despite the fact that it seemed to be an ideal night for cruising and head home, where I attempt to have phone sex over whiskey, but it all becomes too much of a hassle. Can't sleep for a couple of hours (I'm foolishly and needlessly imagining narrow responses on your part to my confession of earlier in the evening. How could I have ever doubted you?), but I finally drift off.

Tuesday I'm feeling much better. I pull out the clippers and trim all of my body hair down to about 1/4 of an inch, shave my balls relatively smooth, and am feeling pretty good about myself. The day is beautiful so I decide a day trip to Blue Cut Canyon is in order. Put on my cum-stiffened jockstrap (I've shot every solo load into it since I returned from you), my ripped to shreds Levi shorts, and a Donald Duck T-shirt.

Blue Cut is beautiful and busy. First I take an olive-complected married man behind some shrubbery and suck on his dark, half-hard cock while he snorts Rush. He insists on sucking on mine, so I let him for a few minutes. He deep throats surprisingly well. I'm back to his, and we take turns like this for about twenty minutes. Finally I tell him that I really want him to shoot his load all over my face. He smiles and agrees, so I sit on my heels with face upturned while he

jacks his cock to orgasm. He directs most of his jism onto my partially opened mouth, and I lick what I can from my lips and wipe the
rest off with the tissue I've got wadded up in my pocket.

The next trick is very similar to the last in appearance--dark
complexion, black buzzed hair, and sexy Italian features. This one
also sports a wedding ring, but is not in the slightest bit interested in
reciprocating. Even better. His cock is also very long and uncut. We
cross the stream for privacy, and I suck on him for what seems like
eternity. At times he'll grab my hair and slide my head back and forth
over his cock, but whenever I gag, he becomes worried and pulls his
cock out. When he finally decides to cum, he pulls out and jacks his
cock over my open mouth while I stare into his reflective sunglasses.
Every so often I place my lips around his cock head while he palms
his shaft, but at the last minute he pivots 45 degrees away and spills
his (my) hard-earned seed onto the sand. I'm miffed. He scuttles
away like a man with a secret, and I pull my jock and shorts back up
while I watch the sand absorb his ropes of cum.

My next adventure is with a huge, burly, bald black man with a
fat uncut cock. He's tattooed with women's names in what strikes
me as amateur, prison-style pen and needle work. I've sucked him
before so we chat a minute before I go down on the cock protruding
from his boxers. A drunken menace comes to watch and participate,
but I do my best to shoo him away. My burly friend comes quickly,
however, and he also wastes his load on the ground.

Soon after that I'm sucking a very veiny and thick and long cock
tortured with rubber rings at the base of the shaft, belonging to a
young man in a purple tank top and Levi shorts. I perform for an
audience of two who grab my tits, lick my ass cheeks and try to

suck my dick while I'm worshipping this beautiful cock wielded by a boy standing on a rock. In order to avoid a repeat of the last two tragedies, I give the boy explicit instructions to shoot his load onto my face. He agrees and soon complies. He's worried about the cum on my eye: "I know how that feels and it burns like hell. I'm r eally sorry." I tell him not to worry, that it's a risk worth taking.

I wander down to the stream again where I'd noticed some sun-bathers earlier. I spot a beautiful nude man reclining in a lawn chair set smack in the middle of the stream, and through the rushes and cat-tails, I can detect some groping of the groin. I walk closer, and see his very fine cock at full, almost erupting, erection. And what's more, with every stroke, he is producing yet another large, sticky drop of pre-cum. I talk to him about the weather a bit, notice his Marine tat-toos and shaved balls, and soon I'm stepping out of my own clothes. I'm completely naked on the shore, and walk through the water toward his mouth-watering hard-on. We take turns sucking one another, and he's turned on by the fact that I'll slurp up pre-cum as quickly as he can produce it. Once again, I decide to be explicit about what my goals are. After squirting all over my face, he pauses to admire my visage, covered with his glistening jism. I kiss the last of the cum from his cock head and lick what I can from around my mouth, as far as my tongue will extend. He gives me a drink of water from his thermos and we talk more about sunbathing at Blue Cut before

I dress and wend my way to my car.

Today I may head into West Hollywood with a friend who's in high hopes of meeting again the dyke of her dreams at the Abbey. I'll take my epistolary novel to read between boy-watching, but I expect no action today.

Once again I thank you for your very sweet and unassuming letter to me--I'm longing for you more than ever. Now as I think about all the things I have yet to do, and you accompany me always. I've never had anyone haunt my imagination as persistently as you have.

Again, I love you.

Paul

--- ▶ ---

FROM: PAUL

DATE: WEDS, MAR 27

Kevin,

I've been going nonstop it seems since yesterday morning, and I finally have a moment to write you and catch you up on the seamier details of my life.

My job Saturday morning was to clean a perfectly clean condo while Bruce, a merchandise wholesaler, did his paperwork, also nude, and watched me clean his kitchen and bathroom floors. He looked to be in his early 50s, wishing he were 30, and he was queeny but friendly. Fed me pizza and iced tea, and we ended with a mutual j.o. session. I sucked on him some, but jerking off really seemed to be his cup of tea. $10 tip, and then I drove home.

My roommate's birthday party was small but lively. Beth and I made a green cake with lavender frosting, and at about ten we all decided to head out to Palm Springs. Robert met the love of his life (about the fourth since I've known him), and spent the evening mooning over him. The others left around one a.m., so I headed over to the adult bookstore next to the bar where we'd been. Immediately I have the great fortune to meet up with a very attractive, nasty-looking young man-tall, goatee and about seven earrings per ear. I follow him into his large and plush video booth, and am sucking on his cock--a fine-sized specimen--in no time. His balls are shaved and he has a small horseshoe-shaped ring pierced through the scrotum just below the shaft of his cock. Both his tits are also pierced, and he is nearly hairless all over. He loves standing on the cushioned benches that line three of the booth's walls, and I alternated between sucking his cock and licking his very smooth, very soft asshole. He has kicked one leather boot off, and freed his leg from his pants and underwear so that he can squat over my face while I rim him. He has a dirty mouth to boot, so I have great fun servicing this wild stud. He fucks me for a while as well, but soon I'm back on my knees, my face in the warm, wet crack of his ass lapping at his hole like an animal. Rimming him sends him over the top, and he steps back to cum--I position my mouth just an inch or so away from his cock head, and he jerks his cum into my open mouth. I especially like that he doesn't close or avert his eyes from my face for a second while he orgasms. He thanks me. We clean up in the bathroom together. I head back over to the bar, but Robert and his true love are still being giddy over one another on the patio, so I ask them if they plan to hang around for a while longer. They do, so I head back over to the video shop. First I find a hung daddy figure who needs his cock sucked, so he and I enter a booth where I repeatedly choke on his horse-dick while he shoves it down my throat relentlessly. How I'd love for you to teach me to suppress my persistent gag-reflex! Oh well, some guys love the sound of a guy choking on their cocks. The hung daddy also loves to squeeze his balls and watch me lick his nuts, which I'm happy to do as well. He starts cumming unexpectedly, but luckily I've taken my

T-shirt off, so his load rains down all over my chest. I rub his jism over my torso, get dressed, and wander back into the merchandise area to see who else I might help out.

I make eye contact with a mustached man whose eyes are at half-mast. I worry that he's really drunk, but he's attractive and interested, so we head to another booth. He can't get the video machine to accept his ragged bills, so we ignore the screens and I start to suck on his dick while he sits back on the bench. He's overly sensitive and claims I'm using teeth when I know I'm not. His cock is very thick and he gets close a few times, but really wants to watch me cum, and I don't want to yet. I rim him for a while, and he fucks me for a few minutes, but when his cock pops out of my ass, it's covered in shit. I hate this--I'm normally very clean, but you never know when fucking will lead to this minor unpleasantness. I head to the restroom and bring him some tissue. He's no longer in the mood and I'm afraid he's mad at me, but instead he tells me to meet him outside by his truck in a few minutes. He cleans up in the restroom, and we meet in the parking lot. I tell him I can't go home with him because my friend is in the bar next door, but he just wants to give me his phone number. I take it, promising to call, but I'm pretty sure that I won't.

Back at the bar, Robert is ready to part from his Romeo, so we head home and I get to sleep at around four a.m. I sleep until after noon, however, and spend the rest of the day on work. Eat burritos and go with friends to see Fargo--terrific film.

And now it's evening, and I'm heading off to bed wishing you and I were taking turns with that pierced rough boy from LA. I know we could have coaxed a load for each of us--and then we would have roamed the video store till dawn using our mouths to pleasure all the men we chose. I'd meet you outside the booth where you'd just sucked off a satisfied stud, hold your head in my hands, and, with my tongue, lick the stray streak of cum from you chin, place it back in your mouth where it belongs.

Last night driving across the desert, I spotted the comet, and of course I thought of you. A good omen, let's say? I'm so happy my spring break has arrived, but I wish to that comet I could spend just a bit of it with you. Write soon and tell me about your weekend adventures. I'll have my cock and palm poised and ready.

Paul

--- ▶ ---

FROM: KEVIN
DATE: WEDNESDAY, MARCH 27, MIDNIGHT
Paul,

I loved your letter about the sandy sex of Blue Cut Canyon. I'll have to revise my condescending city-mouse opinion of the provinces—you're clearly well supplied with opportunities for anonymous debauchery. Better, I warrant, than I am here. In a region where so many places are queer, few are truly thronged. The sex is spread too thin.

I wish I had something meaty to report, but my day was tediously chaste. I feel beset by work and small commissions, on the eve of the arrival of an old boyfriend and his husband. Both dreading and looking forward to it. I field a few calls from potential tricks, but this is too much like dating or interviewing for work; we exchange qualifications and requirements, then discuss availability. There's much to be said for accosting men in dark parks or among whispering reeds. No preliminaries.

I'm adrift. I want to tell people about you, but I don't. I guard you jealously. I see my drawn reflection in the window of a train or bus, sitting beside pretty youths, and I know that I am not worthy of you. I remember your hard cock in my mouth. I hope I dream tonight of your cock in my mouth.

Kevin

--- ▶ ---

FROM: KEVIN
DATE: THURSDAY, MARCH 28, AFTER MIDNIGHT
Paul,
Well, so far, so good. My houseguests are arrived safely; happy, bossy as ever--but this time, on my turf. I'm committed to making a bella figura in every way as host. Perhaps the greatest hardship will be sleep deprivation, as they're sure to want to get up at the crack of dawn each day. I do enjoy immersing myself in the French language again.

Managed to squeeze in some cocksucking today, amidst frenetic housecleaning. Daniel, a guy who apparently rents himself out as an escort, said he liked my ad. Mid-20s, dark Italian looks, big gym chest, nice fur pattern. Face fluctuated between glamorous-handsome and boyish-goofy. He stripped and ordered me to work. Nothing special in the dick and balls category, surprising for a rent boy, but verbal and firm. At one point he instructed me to stick out my tongue and hold my mouth wide open as he fucked my face. Made for noisy slurps and immediate gagging. He fucked my throat as I lay on my back, and liked to have his balls sucked and licked. He would have liked to be rimmed, but was too polite to insist when I didn't make it down there on my own. Most obliging about cumming on my face and in my open mouth, as I lay again on my back and he jacked off with the head of his dick in my face. I sucked the last of the semen out of him afterward. My eye stung for a while--yes, cum. He was in no hurry to leave, so we talked, my head in his lap. Wanting to acknowledge his professional status in a friendly way, I got up to give him a $20 bill, which pleased him though he protested he hadn't expected anything. We parted cheerfully. He stuck his thumb in my mouth to say good-bye.

My very eligible friend Scotty was here this evening, to have dinner and collect the Frogs from SFO. He bemoaned the fact that he had exchanged many fervent looks with a beautiful guy at a lunch but that neither was able to take the next step. Why is it so hard to flirt? It mystifies me, but I know it's true for most of us. But it's strange that it should be so difficult. It reminds me though that I am indeed taken, ought to be hors de combat, and that you deserve the attentions of someone who isn't already mired in marriage. You deserve the best. Until you find him, though, I beg you to let me serve you.

Kevin

--- ▸ ---

FROM: KEVIN
DATE: FRIDAY, MARCH 29
Paul
What a day. Exhausted, and these guys will run me ragged tomorrow. I want my usual nine hours' sleep. God I crave you.

K

--- ▸ ---

FROM: KEVIN
DATE: SATURDAY, MARCH 30, 6:00 P.M.

Paul

I ditched the houseguests. I was so traumatized and wiped out by our outing yesterday that I woke up at four a.m. and couldn't get back to sleep until 7:30. Relived some of the day's little outrages--staring, 6' away, arm pointing, declaring (in French, but still): "Look at the cute kid. Take her picture," while the other obliged with a phallic camera in her face; or brazenly suggesting that I should give them photographs again--because they like it, from me it's free, and someday it may be worth something. Their lack of tact astonishes me. It's not just a cultural thing. All the other Europeans I know are super sensitive. These guys are nothing so much as old-fashioned Ugly Americans. They even wear near-matching warm-up suits in purples and blues, fin de siècle leisure suits. Way too Mall-of-America. Then, they bicker. The most transparent silly vicious married-people kind of sniping--a grotesque caricature of George and me.

I invented, then, a case of food poisoning and sent them off alone. Too much a coward to challenge them any more directly.

Seeing my ex-boyfriend, though, reminds me of our good times together, especially good sex. I was 20 and he 28 when we met in a public park, on practically my first night there as a foreign student. We were boyfriends all year, both fairly grown up about the situation. Neither was jealous of the other; he worried that I had settled on him too soon. Anyway, I messed around with plenty of others and besides, he drew us into three-ways all the time. No homo-boy buddy of mine was safe, he accosted them all. Tried with the stray straight boy too. As much as I resisted all definition--even discussion--of myself as a bottom, I was decidedly his minion. I was much taller than he was, but he was older, more experienced, had a huge dick, and was determined to use it. The vanilla sex I would have been happy with was not enough for him. He almost always wanted to fuck me, and for all my natural resistance I always let him. I've never been a groaner, and can maintain near silence in bed (memories of public encounters or grandparents down the hall), but with Armand I was a moaner. The walls shook, I moaned rhythmically, and my neighbor Elisa upstairs always knew when I was getting it. I even greased myself once, secretly, with an anesthetic cream, then had to confess and explain why his boner was going numb. It was with him that I experimented for the only time with piss—he pissed on me and in me, advised me to stop drinking the bitter stuff. And it was with Armand that I did my only fisting, pumping most of my hand in his small round butt, enjoying the feeling of complete power to instigate sensation, and to inflict pain. Both scenes, of course, were his idea. He seemed made for sex, with his tireless, fat, long uncut cock. Short, yes, but formed of tight swelling curves, perfect ass, permanent tan, smooth skin, black almond eyes—almost Samoan in aspect. A fixed piercing look that said: sex.

I discovered in public gardens that European foreplay consists of a firm hand on the crown of the head, pushing down toward the crotch. Nothing makes me happier now; it made me very angry at the time. The pigs! What made them think they were such top dogs and I such an unter-whelp? Because I was young? Slender? Foreign looking? not über-dogish in my face or facial expression? Time after time, though, they surprised me. If I shook my head when they slapped my butt and wanted to fuck me with a bit of saliva, half the time they'd

spit on my dick and back into me. Guys who wouldn't suck my dick
were delighted to stick their tongues up my ass—attempted lube, of
course. Go figure. Sexy people, though. European men, especially the
Italians, are a miraculous race, oozing testosterone, more beautiful
than they have any right to be. It wasn't that long ago that some
Britons and Frenchmen were curiously scrawny and unprepossessing.
You could think: they're still recovering from WWII, they've only
recently discovered the joys of dentistry and daily bathing. But the
Italians, somehow, were then and are now as sexy as gods.

Thank you for your photograph. Your smile is so beautiful, you are
so good-looking, that I turn back to the image again and again.
Already it's propped on my desk, and will stay. George asked about it,
and I reminded him who you were. He agreed you are handsome, and
said he hoped I would see you again. I've mentioned you in passing, he's
always responded with a very correct indulgence. Of course I don't
want to outrage or hurt him. Along the same lines, I've realized that I
have been leaving very obvious computer trails lying around. It's possible that he's read some or all of this. I can't help feeling somewhat
constrained by this, but on the other hand I am determined to go
ahead. It may be foolish of me, foolish to fall in love by letter with a
beautiful young man, foolish and cruel to the beloved (who deserves
someone, as I said before, unattached and better than I), and cruel,
potentially, to George. Then I'll be a fool. I'll be damned if I'll renounce
the feelings I harbor for you. My heart, head and cock all pine for you,
take comfort in the idea of you, wish you all happiness.

Kevin

--- ▶ ---

FROM: KEVIN
DATE: SUNDAY, MARCH 31, LATE

Paul,

I knew full well you were off to Los Angeles this weekend with your friend who is casing UCLA, but somehow I forgot and have been pining for you all weekend, calling you and hanging up before the machine kicks in. I think it was the arrival of your photo. I look at it and want to devour your. The presence of my exasperating Gauls, too, must have something to do with it. At any event, at the moment your line is busy.

Nothing sexy to report, except this: saw a fairly good-looking, apparently robust, even clean beggar in front of a neighborhood store. Around 30, well built, white, unmistakably heterosexual. Seemed more a drifter than hardcore homeless type. Anyway, I liked his looks. I wrote him a note: shower, $20, best blowjob you've ever had, today or tomorrow? And gave it to him with 50¢. Laughed to myself and at myself later, in pleasure at being so outrageous, in bemusement at my stupidity. And, guess what, he called later. Asked first if it was a serious offer. Said he was interested in the money; protested that no, it wasn't such a weird note. Actually sounded like a decent guy—at least not disdainful of his potential John. I told him I couldn't get together until noon Wednesday, and to call then. We'll see. If I'm found cut into little pieces in a Berkeley dumpster, contact authorities.

Your phone's still busy. I'll send this off.

Kevin

FROM: PAUL

DATE: MON, APR 1

Kevin

I'm still reeling after our phone conversation today. You make me superbly happy, and your sexy voice keeps my cock rock hard throughout our conversations. I want so badly to lie next to your naked body all afternoon today and run my fingers through your pubic hair and over your testicles.

I still have to catch you up on a couple of public sex adventures I had this weekend. Friday afternoon I took a trip to Blue Cut where I ran into the Mexican hunk who nearly twisted my right tit off a while back. He was sunbathing on the far side of the creek—completely nude with a metal cock ring keeping his uncut, veiny cock in an impressive erection. He motioned for me to come over to his spot, so I crossed the creek and undressed. We weren't too secluded so anyone passing by would have had a complete view of our ensuing antics, but no one bothered us. I sucked his cock in a variety of positions--my favorite being his standing up, clutching a handful of my hair from the top of my head, and furiously ramming his swollen cock into my throat. After the cocksucking, he swathed his cock in condoms and began to fuck the hell out of me. He came while pounding my ass dog-style, but didn't pull out, and stayed hard. I asked him to cum again, so he began to fuck me anew, and filled his condom with another load of cum. I didn't orgasm, and instead dressed and headed home to make my dinner date with my lesbian friends.

Later that night, after pizzas and X-Files with the lesbians, I was feeling incredibly horny, so I headed to the park, but was aching for a more exciting venue. I'd seen an ad in Frontiers for a new sex club

in Palm Springs called The Gravel Pit--a promising name--so instead I
headed into the desert at eleven p.m.

Small detour at the rest stop just outside of PS and sucked a load
of cum out of a daddy's cock. The Gravel Pit was disappointingly
slow when I arrived, although I occupied myself with licking the
largest nuts I'd ever encountered and sucking on the half-hard cock
that accompanied them. Soon a cowboy with a monster cock
arrived, and I gagged his schlong down my throat while his friend
worked his nipples. He got ready to come, so I positioned my face
just under his cock head, and he squirted a fierce load all over my
open-mouthed face. I walked to the restroom to see myself in the
mirror, and had plenty of admiring glances from men staring at my
cum-drenched beard and lips.

Two more loads adorned my face before the evening was out--I
simply rubbed each one into my beard and face so that I could constantly smell and/or taste the jizz as I chose. The highlight of the
evening, however, was a small German boy with a disturbingly large
and uncut cock whom I found with an older man who was mercilessly
twisting the young foreigner's nipples. I immediately took the boy's
arching cock into my mouth, and tasted his plentiful ooze. Soon we
were both naked, and I kept his cock at the back of my throat while
he intermittently fucked my face. He exploded into my mouth, and I
swallowed every drop of his cum, but refrained from shooting my own
load. I asked him if he ever got into piss, and he said he did. "Could
you piss now?" I asked, looking at his still mostly-turgid cock.

"I'm not sure," he replied, "but I'll try." I dropped to my kne es,
spread my legs wide enough to keep me below his shaft, and within
seconds, the boy began to piss into my mouth. I swallowed three

sizable mouthfuls--very bitter and acidic, but wildly erotic to take
fluid from a man's cock into my gulping mouth. But the boy shows no
signs of stopping! I can swallow no more, so I let him piss over my
face, and it runs off my beard and onto my chest and groin. Every so
often I lap at the incessant stream that continues from his hardening
cock, and eventually I bend my head down, and let him piss over my
back and ass. I am amazed at how much piss this little man is holding. He must be all bladder, because he urinates for what feels like
an eternity, then somehow the stream subsides, and he pants over
his reeking, debased pig boy. I tell you no lie when I say that I've
NEVER seen (or heard) a man piss as long as my German did all over
me. He dresses and thanks me sheepishly; I haul my butt to the
men's room where I do my best to clean myself with paper towels
and water. I'm the last to leave the Gravel Pit at four a.m., and giggle
to myself all the way home at what a fucking slut I've been tonight.

   Piss is becoming more and more important to me. I thrill at the
image of a well-built man holding his plump cock toward my mouth,
and groaning with pleasure as a stream of piss erupts from his
cock head and hits me full on the face, dripping into my mouth and
over my beard. I fantasize that I have a master/daddy who visits
my house on a regular basis for service. That I keep a six pack of
beer in the fridge for him, and that when he calls and wants to
come over, I'm waiting for him in white briefs, on my knees in the
kitchen with the door unlocked. He walks in, secures my hands
behind my back with a cord, and helps himself to a cold beer. He
forces me to drink some of it, and eventually reclines back in a
chair and orders his boy to piss in his underpants. I concentrate but
can't pee. He becomes impatient and pours more beer down my

throat, and prods me to urinate. Finally I feel myself relaxing and a
hot load of bright yellow piss begins to soak my briefs, making my
underwear nearly transparent and running down my thighs. Now my
master/father stands above me, pulls his own fat cock from his fly
and lets loose a long-pent-up stream of urine into my face, my
hair, over my chest, and onto my already soaked underwear.
Placing his still pissing cock deep into my mouth, he sprays the
last of his piss down my throat. His cock swells and fills my
mouth, and he begins to pump himself back and forth into my face.
He grips the back of my head, and his testicles swing back and
forth against my chin. Without intermission, he pounds his cock
into my face until his thick cum spurts from his piss-slit and coats
the interior of my mouth and throat. I swallow it down, and he
flicks the last of his load onto my lips and chin. He buttons his fly,
thanks me for the beer, and leaves his piss-covered boy on his
knees on the floor with a rock hard hard-on raging in his wet briefs.

So do you have any takers for this fantasy? You could even take
photos of the scene, and shoot your own load all over my well-used
face as a coda. Or if you want to play the role of piss-daddy, you're
more than welcome, Kevin....

Now I really have to go jerk off--I'll have you in mind while I pull
the cum from my dick, and taste it as a tribute to my fuck-
buddy/lover/friend who inspires me to plunge further and further
into gorgeous depths of depravity. A small and insufficient means of
worshipping you.

Paul

--- ▶ ---

>d.o.c.

FROM: KEVIN

DATE: MONDAY, APRIL 1, 6:00 P.M.

Paul,

Thanks for calling me today. It's a maudlin cliché, but I love you
so much that it feels like my heart will burst. I'm restless,
craving you, plotting ways to see you. My obsession of the
moment includes taking you to Paris and Italy. I want to drown
you with beauties of place, with oysters and caviar, with uncut
Latin cocks. Think about getting a passport. I will contrive to
somehow get the money to pay for both of us. Are you done with
classes in June?

The day's sex-business: Phone sex with a Japanese-German guy
who wants to suck dicks with me, haven't met him yet. Paged a
new guy, straight 32 year old who wants to be serviced, delightful-
ly uptight and butch. Think I seduced him with my usual baritone
rumblings: that I've only connected with a few guys this way
(yeah, right), but that most have been straight/bi/married/what-
ever; that there are a lot more guys out there getting or wanting
a great blowjob from another guy than anybody cops to; that men
want it for all kinds of reasons—some just appreciate great
technique; some are so horny that they have to stick it somewhere; that I may not be Uma Thurman, but I am handsome enough
for a guy; and some straight guys like to see their dicks disappear down my throat. None of this is very modest on my part, but
I'm acting as soft-sell lobbyist, cajoling the heterosexual cock
into my mouth.

Will you tell me more about the time that you first became a
cumdrinker? I am greedy for everything associated with you,

your history, everything.

    More soon,

    Kevin

--- ▶ ---

FROM: PAUL

DATE: TUES, APR 2

Kevin,

When I was 13 and living a million miles from anywhere in benighted
Midwestern suburbs, I was desperate to know more about what I
later came to know and call gay sex. I'd had my first experience in a
public library with a man at least ten years my senior. I told you and
George about this over breakfast, but it amounted to the two of us
groping one another next to a dumpster. In any case, I wanted to
talk with other men who might be into such same-sex gropings, so I
asked my adolescent self: What kind of men would want to have sex
with other men? Somehow photographers seemed to be the logical
answer, and so, after I'd return home from junior high school I
would go through our Yellow Pages and call photographers' studios.
My opening line was "What kind of underwear are you wearing?" I
was really into underwear ads (as I've explained before), and I fig-
ured that any man who bothered to answer such a random and bold
question would be bound to be interested in men's underwear (and
what such clothing houses).

    Most of my photographers were disgusted, amused, or simply
hung up with no comment. But one in particular was quite impressed
with my query, and we talked a long time about what it meant to
lust after men, and their bodies. This photographer had shot a series

>85

of semi-pornographic pics of boys and men in their underwear or in athletic gear. He wanted to shoot a series of photos of me, but he had no idea how old I really was. I think I told him I was 16 or 17. He told me a remarkable story about a gymnast friend of his who would hang suspended, gripping a high bar, and rub his legs together. This would excite him to the point of orgasm, and this photographer loved to watch the cum stain spread over the groin of his friend's athletic pants. I called this photographer frequently, and he always answered my questions frankly and seductively.

When we moved to Arizona, I discovered that gay bars existed in the Phoenix area. I began to call bartenders--afternoons were always good times to call, as the bars were less busy--and some were very happy to talk to me. One bartender would pass the receiver to various clients who would talk dirty to me, and I would beat myself off to their sordid stories and propositions. One bartender in particular was very sexy over the phone. He always claimed to be wearing cut-offs that showed off his large cock nicely. While talking dirty to me and breathing heavy, he claimed he was rubbing his crotch up against the bar, and would hump the bar until he released a load into his jeans and down his leg. He told me that the customers at the bar found this very exciting, and if I remember correctly I talked to some of these and confirmed my bartender-friend's claims.

Meanwhile, I would collect the phone numbers of clients from the bars who didn't mind my calling them at home. I never wrote these down, but memorized them. At one point, I probably had 20 different numbers committed to memory, and this provided me with a pretty reliable source of phone sex opportunities. One fellow left the receiver of his telephone against his TV speakers while he played a

videocassette of a particularly verbal porno; at the other end, I
jacked off to the heavy breathing and filthy voice--both reeking of
sex and sweat and cum. Once, I got out of bed in the middle of the
night, and called a man I'd talked with before. My parents must have
suspected that I was making dirty phone calls to men in the middle
of the night, because they had left the receiver off the hook in their
bedroom, and heard the sound of me dialing in the kitchen. I ran to
my room, but my father came and sat on my bed, asking me who I
was calling in the middle of the night. I pretended to be delirious--
that I had been walking in my sleep, and that I had no idea what he
was talking about. I was terrified.

All though high school, I had phone sex on an average of at least
once a week, so when I discovered real phone sex lines (the ones
that charge you!), I was immediately seduced into calling these.
While I was with my ex, I once racked up over a hundred dollars in
phone sex charges. He was horrified, and thought (still thinks) I was
a hopeless sex-addict, a pervert who had no concept of money.

These lines were less spontaneous and much more codified in
terms of how phone sex conversations ensued, but it was the place
I began to let my imagination run wild with S/M, bondage, piss, and
spanking fantasies--all of which I've now had the good fortune to
enact in the flesh. I'm not much into phone sex now, but I have to
admit that this afternoon I called a man in Sherman Oaks who talked
me through an orgasm--he was a daddy very intent on being serviced by a boy who would swallow whatever his father's dick produced. But as a student I have to watch my phone bill, so phone sex
has taken a back seat to tearoom and park cruising, which cost only
a minimal amount of gas money.

>d.o.c.

I'll tell you about my first cum-drinking experience again next post. I've got to get some sleep. I can still hear your lovely voice in my ears, and I want so badly to feel your lips against them while you whisper filthy words to me, one hand round my balls, the finger of your other hand probing my hungry asshole. It takes just a little bit of thinking about you to make my cock throb...but of course I think about you constantly.

Paul

--- ▶ ---

FROM: KEVIN
DATE: TUESDAY, APRIL 2
Paul,

Spurred by your piss-drenched posting, the mental image of your beard dripping with cum, I cycled off to the baths last night. Hadn't been since the night we met. Found a fair amount of "movement" for a Monday night. Quickly got a tall, severe, 30-ish guy's normal-sized dick in my mouth. He pounded away nicely for a while. Sensing that he wasn't ready to come, I grabbed his dick in my hand and gave his glans a good-bye slurp.

In the arena, I approached a black-haired, fair-skinned late 20s type who was pressed flat against a glory hole wall, being sucked by a guy in a booth below. His white round butt looked great flexing on his tensed legs. After just a moment of my stroking his butt he pulled out of the other guy's mouth, glanced my way, and disappeared. I felt jinxed—I'd just been turned down by a big-dicked guy. Didn't like the idea that by intruding, ever so tactfully, on somebody else's scene, I had broken their spell. It's a delicate matter, offering

to join a pair already mutually engaged. In a few moments though,
as I stood in full view on the floor of the room, black-haired guy
was back, standing above me at the railing, offering me his big
hard-on. Compact black bush, long, slightly down-curved, cock
pointed right at my mouth, I started deep-throating him and quickly got into a cocksucking trance state. Ran my hands all over his
well-proportioned, thickset curves. After a good long session he
shot noisily down my throat.

After some fleeting contacts, hooked up with a big farmboy
(learned later) from Bakersfield. Around 30, tall and broad-shouldered, studly but not buffed, nice mushroom-head dick. Sucked him
in the privacy of a dark booth for quite a while, before telling him I
would love to take his load later. Ended up sucking another guy, late
20s, looked exactly like a younger Mr. Clean, down to shaved head,
shit-eating smile, and earring. His entire body was shaved clean,
perfectly muscled in regulation porn-star proportions, tanned gold
as only blondes can be. He was as happy to suck as he was to be
sucked, and in 69ing he made wonderful slurping noises as he
sucked me with gulping, quick-lapping motions like a calf at the
teat. He was fun, avid, and very complimentary to your humble
friend, who certainly didn't feel his equal. Good kisser too. His quite
big uncut blond cock, narrower at the head, stayed hard the whole
time, whether I was pumping it down my throat or just toying with
it as I knelt over his face and fucked his mouth.

On further wanderings, witnessed black-haired guy being sucked
by a fat guy who manipulated him to a climax that shot three feet-
-wanted to jump in and take it, but didn't. Found farmboy in a booth
sucking someone through a hole, and quickly got on my knees to

suck him while he worked on the other. The disembodied cock came on farmboy's face and in his mouth, he in turn came on me.

All night I dreamt of writing and relating these experiences to you, composing real-life porn passages in my sleep. And as for travel plans, the entire thing is absurd of course. Even so, I can't help thinking, planning, scheming for it somehow. There is so little I can give you that reflects the importance you hold for me. If only I could have found you in Phoenix, when we were both kids. How I would have made love to you, taught you how to suck dick, fucked you for hours with your ankles on my shoulders, your thighs against my chest, our tongues locked, my gaze as deep in your green-blue eyes as my cock in your tight little hole. How we would fall asleep with my dick in your ass, with our dicks in each other's mouths. How I would ply you with beer, then refuse to let you piss, your bladder aching, while my own piss splashed in a heavy stream from your open mouth onto your tender naked chest. How I would lick my piss and cum off your face and cover every inch of you with kisses. These things I can't give the 13-year-old Paul. Now that I'm old and fucked, and you at your beautiful prime, I still offer you all the sexual worship in my limited means.

Kevin

--- ▶ ---

FROM: KEVIN
DATE: TUESDAY, APRIL 2, MIDNIGHT
Paul,

Went to my photo group. The model was uninspiring, a Pillsbury Muscle Boy, a doughy bulldog. My shots of him were OK though. As usual, I used the excuse of going into town to go also to the fleshpots. Campus the-

ater, again. Why, why do I go? Eight or ten ugly/boring/antique characters rattling around two stories of filthy chambers. Found an
acceptable face to stick my dick into, let a few of the clientele gather
around. Made myself available to the only good-looking guy there, who
never took me up on it. Eventually acquiesced to the attentions of a
fairly sexy young dad type--tall, nice body, medium-large schwanz. He
ordered me around nicely and made me beg for it, finally coming all
over my face and chest. I had taken my shirt off, and as much as I
liked being creamed on, he wasn't completely my cup of jiz, so I
rubbed my lips over his oozing head, but didn't imbibe.

The main thing that gives me pleasure at the moment is you. It
is a privilege to love you, and I send you loving thoughts all the
time. In conversations with good friends today I was continually distracted by the impulse to divulge all. I didn't, though. There would
be such pleasure in telling others about you, but I also love having
this huge beautiful secret.

Kevin

--- ▶ ---

FROM: PAUL
DATE: WEDS, APR 3
Kevin,
I'm glad to hear you went back to our stomping grounds and sucked
a few for me. I wish I'd been with you, alternately accosting men
together and roaming off alone to find new meat. I saw that flights
to SF are down to $29 one way right now, and my tax return could
show up any day....

I never did give you the scoop about Sunday morning at the

Melrose Baths. My friend and confidant Mike (he lives in Salt Lake City, was a real whore for a couple of years, and is every bit as debauched as you or I) came to visit me in January, and one night after partying in WeHo, we headed to the Melrose Baths and delighted in debasement until the wee hours of the morning. So I still had my membership, and since I wasn't able to see my friend Jan until the afternoon, I decided to head to the baths on a beautiful sunny Sunday morning knowing full well that I had only a few hours at most to spare. Right away I ran across dark-haired, thick ear-ringed Rich who was there with his lover, Luke. They'd come from a leather party that lasted all night, and I suspected that they were trying to come down off of something. Rich was a dirty talker, which kept my attention, and we took turns sucking on one another's cocks in full view of everyone traversing the video room. We discussed our mutual and fairly recent fondness for piss sex, and Rich began to be antsy to get fucked. I told him I'd just arrived, so I wanted to roam a bit, but that I'd search him out later. This is how I get out of having to fuck. He seemed disappointed and unconvinced that I'd keep my word, but resigned himself. No one else caught my eye, and the whirlpool was being drained--I was really in the mood to relax in a hot tub for a little while.

I found Rich again, and we headed for the steam room, where we made out and he worked a finger up into my ass. He suggested a three-way with his lover, which I assented to, but Luke never materialized. Soon I was baking, and Rich's earrings were so hot that they burned me whenever I brushed a hand or my lips against them, so we went upstairs to the group labyrinth. Here we tried fucking, but as soon as Rich was in me, a crowd of men closed in on us, and we both lost our hard-ons from all the claustrophobic thronging. We headed to another part of the maze, but soon I was being sucked by a massive gentleman with a very tight grip and he worked a finger into my asshole while a newly reformed mass of flesh began to push in on me from all sides, stroking my legs, slapping my ass, tugging at my tits. I tried to wrench myself free from the persistent and powerful cocksucker at my groin, but he only became a human vise, and swallowed my ready-to-burst cock even further down his throat. "I'm going to cum," I said, and desperately tried to fr ee myself so as not to explode into the man's mouth, but to no avail: I began to shoot, and had to practically fight to get his mouth off my overly sensitive dick. Rich was thoroughly disappointed that I'd spent a load in someone else's mouth, but I told him to hold tight, and we'd see what I could do later.

I went to the roof-patio to sun for a bit, and sure enough Rich fol-lowed me out and we chatted about his life for a while. I found a pay phone and called my friend Jan who was eager to see me, so I told Rich that I'd suck him off in the steam room if he'd let me. He agreed, and I took his watery load all over my face. In the shower, I was finally able to cum again, and he was content to have me shoot it onto his thigh. I got his number, and may just call him since he has a good sense of what goes on among the leather folk in Silverlake.

So my first load of cum....

I'd been cruising the humanities building at the college ever since I detected the glory hole in the downstairs men's room while on a date with a girl student. The building is also named for one of my Mormon ancestors, so I always felt as if I had a bit of a right to whatever pleasures it had to offer. During one particular cruising scene in which I'd run across a handsome, serious-looking older man, I found my

partner being fairly forceful with my head and mouth. He would grip
my cranium with his large hand, and direct my tongue and lips over
his testicles and his cock while his coarse pubic hair scrubbed my
face. Soon I was on my back so that he could drop his low-hanging
balls into my mouth and slap my face with his cock. He was verbal in
a sexy young Brando way, and as he brought his meat closer to an
eruption, he asked if he could shoot his cum onto my face. I nodded,
kept my lips slightly parted, and waited for the drops to fall. It was
nearly an out of body experience for me when I felt ropes of warm,
sticky cum begin to drip and spray onto various parts of my face. He
left immediately, embarrassed and guilty I suppose, while I remained
on the bathroom floor looking up into the ceiling lights wishing for a
view of my cum-coated countenance. I did move to admire myself in
the mirror where I extended my tongue and tasted the jism from my
lips. With a forefinger I slid some of the larger deposits to my lips so
that I could taste more. I'd never experienced anything as erotic and
as transgressive as this before, and at that moment I kissed vanilla
sex goodbye forever. I've never gone back, as you well know.

Finding people to cum onto my face--much less into my mouth--
was a bit of a chore at that conservative school. I do recall one
drunken older man who appeared to have been a custodian or
handyman. I sucked on his cock in the same restroom while he
moaned and called me his boy. I stopped only to instruct him that I
wanted him to shoot all over my face, to which directions he replied
quite enthusiastically. When he did cum, he shot a mammoth
amount of semen onto my face while I kept my mouth opened for
whatever might happen to make its way in. I remember walking
immediately to the mirror and standing in awe at what is still the

most cum-covered face I've ever seen. There was hardly any surface that escaped the thick and copious ropes of cum that dripped
into my beard and off my chin. I rubbed the cum into my face and
hair, turned back to my drunken daddy figure, and thanked him for
the semen shower. I refused to wash my face, and walked out of
the restroom with glistening skin, unconcerned about who might
wonder why my face looked well-oiled or who might catch a whiff of
the bleach-like smells coming from my reeking direction.

But now it's back to my studies. Cum to me in my dreams,
Kevin. I could easily save my Europe cherry for you, you know. Any
others you'd like?

They're yours.

Paul

--- ---

FROM: PAUL
DATE: WEDS, APR 3
Kevin,
Just got your package a bit ago, and savored every moment opening
it--more scraps of my much beloved Kevin. I had the juvenile
impulse to start writing your name all over my notebook, to perform
numerology on you and participate in a wide array of goofy, infatu-
ated doodling and daydreaming about you. You're everywhere with
me--I eat food and wonder if you'd like it, drink wine and think how
we need to savor a fine bottle together, check out classical CDs
from the public library and wonder who your favorite composers are,
turn out the light and wish to God that your gorgeous person were
next to me in my lumpy futon bed.

I really must start to read now, I spent too much time yesterday
planning to get work done, and far too little time actually accom-
plishing anything. I'm so tempted to call you again, but I'm afraid of
being a pest, or making a fool of myself over the phone. Worried that
any day you'll become aware of what a disappointment I am. That I'm
in no way worthy of the smallest of your loving touching gestures.

Your books, the wonderful Duane Michaels photo, and the box
these arrived in will go on my dresser next to my bed--a sort of
Kevin shrine where I worship morning and night. I miss you terribly,
and think about you continually. Thank you; I kiss your lips in return.

Paul

--- ▶ ---

FROM: KEVIN
DATE: WEDNESDAY, APRIL 3, MIDNIGHT
Paul,
Remember the hunky drifter I accosted? Finally rendezvoused, and
still taste the nicotine in my mouth and on my lips from his dick.
Named Winston, 6'9", it was like sucking off Paul Bunyan. And fortunately the 34-year-old n'er –do-well had a sturdy, slim body and an
average-sized cock that got hard when I played some straight video
porn. Amazing though how much tobacco had permeated his system.
I tasted it as I sucked his dick but was really struck when the bitter taste just wouldn't go away, no matter how much I brushed my
teeth or how many apples I happened to eat. He said he wouldn't be
able to come, so I let him go pretty soon, which was OK with me. He
said he hoped we would be friends, which meant really that he hoped
he'd get money from me again, and said that he'd never hurt nobody,

the declaration of someone accustomed to being thought dangerous. It was arousing to have a hard dick in my mouth that belonged to a straight roughneck, but maybe the aftertaste is too high a price. And of course he knows where I live if he wants to murder me in my bed, an added frisson.

Last night, leaving the sleazy theater, I emerged into the ugliest quarter of the city to see a bright white nickel-sized full moon hanging in the rich blue sky, the same pale cobalt as the fuzzy ceanothus flowers now blooming in other neighborhoods—places where there are growing things, not the Tenderloin. Tonight the moon is fuller still, a blinding peephole of light, and there was supposed to be a lunar eclipse, but when I went outdoors the moon was intact and unobstructed. Everything—everything beautiful—makes me think of you.

I come back again and again to the mental images you've given me. A boy holding 20-odd phone numbers of men to talk to about sex in his head,—I've never heard of such a thing. What a great idea. What a way to have access to a world of adult sex without having to be there in person. Proof, I think, that smart gay people are smarter than the average run of smart straight people—straight teenagers never have to resort to such challenging survival strategies. Also, what a testament to the kindness of strangers, of bartenders who can cum in their jeans by humping a bar while talking to a needy youth on the phone.

And so to bed. I'm drunk on Pesach wine, and you.

Kevin

--- ► ---

FROM: KEVIN

DATE: THURSDAY, APRIL 4, 9:00 P.M.

Paul,

You're at a second-night Passover supper, so I can't call you to soak up the sound of your voice. No sex today, hélas, so I'll dig up an early chapter in my sexual education. Between braces and moving to the West Coast, by 12 or so I was alone with my frequent masturbations. One of my discoveries, though, was a head shop in a little town near my house. Great place to buy incense, black light posters, tarot cards, under-ground papers. This was where I bought my first copies of Gay Sunshine, Fag Rag, and the Berkeley Barb. Took all my courage to buy them from the sweet fat hippie proprietress. From a Gay Sunshine interview with Allen Ginsburg I heard about the novels of Jean Genet, William Burroughs, and the Marquis de Sade. I tripped out on the idea of Cassidy, Orlovsky, and Kerouac having sex with Ginsburg and Burroughs. I had already found, by chance really, the Greek novels of Mary Renault and Yourcenar's Memoirs of Hadrian. I was well supplied with role mod-els. I masturbated thinking about Alexander of Macedon and Hephaiston, Hadrian and Antinous, Michelangelo and his innamorato Tomaso di Cavaliere. In Renault's version of the Theseus story, the hero asks his troubled son Hippolytus, whom he believes to be merely lovesick: is it a girl or a boy? This struck deeply home. A father, a Hellenic father any-way, could expect his son to fall in love with a boy as readily as a girl. Although I was alone in my queerness, I knew there was a distinguished history of cocksuckers behind me. I read the Symposium and Carmides, reading Plato for the dirty parts. I learned then that homosexual love is, or ought to be, the highest kind, because two men will inspire each other to honorable conduct. More than that I learned that it was simply

a fact, a given; that in their looking-glass world, an Athenian would feel
embarrassed about being interested only in women.

Just as powerful as these romantic men of history and fiction
were the naked men in blurry little black-and-white photos at the
back of the Berkeley Barb: ads for porn, for escorts. Naked men, available to other men! Here too were personals ads. I decided to answer
the local ones. The first was also among the most successful. After
talking on the phone, I cycled to the apartment of a 21-year-old math
student at the local community college––he seemed amazingly grown
up to me. Greeting me at he door he was taken aback to find a 13 year
old, however precocious. He invited me in nonetheless. I managed to
persuade him that I was quite grown up––that is, horny and determined. I was, after all, practically my full adult height and weight: 6′
tall, 140 lbs, masturbating three times a day. Anyway, he was mollified,
and dragged me off to the shower, where we had sex for the first
time. A clean freak, he always wanted to begin by bathing. I generally
didn't mind, and it was very sexy to suck each other's dicks as the
water flowed over our faces. I remember him now as of medium
height, well proportioned, dark haired, nice looking, hairy of chest and
stomach. He had a beautiful up-curving dick; which he self-deprecat-
ingly compared it to mine, which he found as big. He bemoaned being
so furry, though I was fascinated. I had only a small triangle of hair
over my dick. He teased a lock of it out in his fingers and remarked
that it was hair, after all, and like all hair could grow too long. It had
never occurred to me that pubic hair might be cut. Lying on his bed
or on the living room rug, we 69ed for hours. He tried once to fuck
me––I told him I wanted to "Greek", though I barely knew what that
meant. So I lay on my stomach and he pressed down on me. In mount-

ing panic, I felt him push his hard dick more and more insistently all around my asshole. Finally his cock hit home and rammed in, to the hilt, in one thrust. It felt like a burning knife wound. I jumped off his cock with a cry and landed ten feet away. He wanted to try again, but I crawled into his arms, trembling, and told him I couldn't. I wouldn't let anyone try to fuck me for years after that.

I saw him half a dozen times, until I drifted away. He never wanted to take my number, as a security precaution, and let me call him when I wanted. We were both aware of the danger, especially to him. I was naively certain that I would have the strength to stand up for him if we were busted. He talked about being in love still with the boy with whom he'd messed around as a kid; a guy who was now dumpy, married, boring, and 21. Even at the time I thought him obsessive and sad about this: first love is important, but sooner or later you have to get over it and move on. For all his obsession with his no-longer golden-boy, he was no pederast, and treated me like an equal. Our sexual connection was definitely one of mutual regard, perfectly embodied in our hours of mutual sucking.

Another time I responded to the ad of a guy who wanted to be fucked, period. He wasn't kidding. When I let myself into his little bungalow, his ass was high in the air and his face deep in a pillow. I couldn't fuck him for very long, but fortunately a nice-looking Stanford music graduate student arrived and fucked him royally, while I licked the fucker's asshole on each up-thrust. After a time, and definitely with the first guy's blessing (he had another on the way?), the grad student took me in his car to one of the dark places in the hills. There we sucked each other in all the positions his back seat permitted, until the cops rousted us with a flashlight and barked questions.

They got a good look at both of us, naked, the car windows completely fogged up, but satisfied themselves with making us go home.

As I began the eight grade, I repeated to myself, thinking of my math student: I've got a lover! I had my own grown up secret, and was transformed by it. A detested twit the year before, suddenly I was popular. I realized that the social mask—the smile, the straight back—was a self-fulfilling prophecy. Act confident, you become confident. Suddenly people thought I was OK. And, because I was getting laid, I had a real reason to feel cocky. I knew of course that my sexuality was despised, and I suffered every day, worrying about slipping into sissyness, tortured by lust for my classmates and my male teachers, but I had the literary example of heroic gay Athenian tyrannicides, and the memory of the taste of men.

Enough for now. Thanks for listening to this.

Kevin

--- ▶ ---

FROM: PAUL
DATE: SAT, APR 6
Kevin,

I'm finally able to log on to my account, and am relieved to see that everything appears to be as I left it on Wednesday. I'm a little con-fused that from my home computer I don't have the long message in which you recount your 13-year-old's whoring adventures. (I can't believe you were reading such sophisticated and difficult texts at that age—I think I was still reading Nancy Drew and the Hardy Boys.) You see, tonight I really put myself into a spin over not being able to retrieve my messages and having woken you up this morning with such nonsensical babble about how I was worried my e-mail account was somehow not working only made my quandary worse. So I downed a couple of glasses of Chianti really fast, called a friend to moan, and she invited me to use her computer. So I went over to her place earlier this afternoon, successfully logged on to the Internet on her computer, and found you'd sent two messages. Apologies once again for waking you up. I should have known better, but sometimes my frantic desires to have more sensual (i.e., aural/oral) communication with you get the better of me, and this morning I found myself dialing you without thinking very hard about it beforehand.

I'll send a longer post tomorrow (if I can log on that is), and perhaps I'll have something more interesting to report. For now, I'm absolutely relieved to have access to my e-mail again. Being cut off from you at this point would be akin to undergoing an amputation. And to think we haven't known one another even one whole month! In any case, you are the principal source of all my happiness right now, and I constantly swoon, moon, and dream about you. And I want so badly to touch, taste, and kiss you as well.

I just got notice that you've mailed me a post--could you really be on the Internet right now? So close, but so far.

Paul

--- ▶ ---

FROM: KEVIN
DATE: SATURDAY APRIL 6, MIDNIGHT
Paul,
What a relief to have you back. I was trying to be stoic, thinking it would be good for me to be less greedy for news of you. But of

course I was dismayed, and coveted you.

Entertained one new trick today, a black guy named Laney who had exchanged several messages with me. On the phone he was butch and friendly, a nice combination. Perfectly frank about having to schedule his time for being sucked off around seeing his kids. In person he was just as appealing, or more: tall, perfectly built, dark chocolate, bright eyes and smile; personable, verbal, demanding. Beautiful big black dick, heavy velvet balls. Sucking him, in all kinds of positions, was a real treat. After a half hour of enjoyable sucking, he warned me that he was about to cum, as if to let me off the hook, but of course I wanted it all and jammed his full length down my throat in order to feel his cum shoot at my tonsils.

I'm not up to writing you properly, too tired to express myself well. I'm tempted to call you, but don't know if I dare. How I'd like to take you in my arms, to drift off to sleep with you after long kisses.

Kevin

--- ▶ ---

FROM: PAUL
DATE: SAT, APR 6
Kevin,
Earlier this morning I was tempted to call when a message appeared at the bottom of my screen to let me know that I had a new message from you. I'd become suspicious of the Internet though, so I wasn't sure if a lag kept your message from arriving on time, or if you really had sent the message off at nearly one a.m.

>d.o.c.

And I did finally get the message about your adolescent
debaucheries. I have to say, I've never read Renault or Yourcenar,
but they'll be on my list now. Wonderful to think that two dead
European lesbians helped a 13-year-old American boy connect his
precocious cocksucking experiences to the heroic male love among
ancient Greeks and Romans. I'm overwhelmed with desires to do so
many things with you I've never done before. To read Renault with
you in Greece and have you perform Greek on me under an Athenian
full moon. To wander through the Prado while you whisper into my
ear about the artworks you enjoy most. To drink martinis in New
York with you. My fantasies of you often take the form of travel--
possibly because our sun signs, and the combination of them, draw
the two of us into a more romantic sensibility. How we love to over-
load our senses and push our corporeal limits to new limits of
never-before-experienced pleasure.

But now I must get back to work. I may end up in Silverlake
tonight, but I'll long for you there as well. Thanks for putting up with
me and my insanities. I love you.

Paul

PS: I nearly forgot to tell you that I saw Morrissey at A
Different Light in WeHo yesterday. At first I thought he was a
severe wannabe, but a sexy British-accented man posting pro-
mos for his play assured me that it was indeed the king of
whiney self-indulgent 80s pop. My first real--well, "real" is a
word that hardly describes any facet of LA--brush with fame in
the city of angels.

--- ---

FROM: PAUL

DATE: SUN, APR 7

Kevin,

It's after 3:30 a.m. and I'm beat. Quick rundown of the evening:
went to Silverlake with friends. Met Cecile's tearoom-cruising
buddy, Eric, and we all went out for cheap seafood. After dinner we
went to a piano bar and watched elderly fags take turns singing
show tunes and torch songs. Max asked me if I would go to the
bathroom with him, and at first I didn't understand why, but then I
realized that since he didn't have a penis, he wouldn't be able to
stand at a urinal, and he wanted someone to be with him if he needed to be guarded at a stall with no door. The stall did indeed have a
door, though, so there was no problem. I never knew Max as Alice,
and have to constantly remind myself that he is not--or has not
always been--just another cute, queeny guy.

Then the dykes went off to a serious butch/femme affair, so the
boys and I went to explore Cuffs--Silverlake's notorious grope bar. It
was fun, but still early for any serious action, so we stood around
looking at the leather/Levis men and drank beer until it was time to
meet the gals. Later we played Trivial Pursuit--Cecile and I kicked
ass, but Max was apparently upset and sulked for a while afterward.

All the way home I told Maria stories of my missionary experiences in Argentina. I actually imagined that I was telling them to
you, and I began to dream of taking you to my favorite little coastal
fishing town, where we would watch the ominous fog roll in at
nights, listen to the superstitious townsfolk tell us of their daugh-
ters being possessed by evil spirits, and eat fresh abalone with
homemade mayonnaise. Two miles down the coast we would watch

the seals sunbathe on the monolithic rocks that form a gateway to
the ocean, and we would explore the severe cliffs and crevices
where prehistoric-looking fish stare up at us while affixed somehow
to the craggy rock walls.

Sueña conmigo esta noche.

Paul

--- ▶ ---

FROM: KEVIN
DATE: MONDAY, APRIL 8, 1:00 A.M.
Paul,

How happy it made me to talk to you today. I am bursting with
curiosity about your new buzzed incarnation. Maybe I'll get down to
see you before it grows back in. How I'd love to stroke that velvety-
bristly head, in sweet chaste moments, to send you to sleep in the
inviting shade of a hot spring day, or in moments less innocent: to
rub your beautiful cranium while you work a nice big joint.

Speaking thereof, nothing to report but some reluctant (on my
part) phone sex with a certain Charles. Reluctant because I had
already jacked off, thinking of you, and because I haven't met him
face to face yet. Don't know if he's really worth talking dirty to. He
sounds interesting though, half Japanese, half German, 26, fucks
girls, loves to eat big black cock. Go figure.

Thank you for taking me, in fantasy, to your fishing village. How
wonderful it would be to go with you there (or to go with you anywhere). Argentina is really, literally, at the antipodes, and must be
strange and beautiful.

About my precocious queer lit studies: I don't think I understood what I was reading, at least not on first reading. Intimations of sex and homosex were enough. I'd read an entire fat difficult book and miss most of it, happy as long as I got characters to identify with, have crushes on, fantasize about. It did make me a reader, though, and a fantasist. Much of it was luck. A relative heard I liked the Greek myths, so she got me all the Mary Renaults. Jackpot. Other family members knew I liked renaissance art, so they gave me Bomarzo, a modern novel by the Argentinean Mujica-Lainez, about a fictional sixteenth-century Count Orsini, a handsome bisexual hunchback. Found E.M. Forster's Maurice in a paperback edition in a supermarket rack, was able to buy it without attracting too much attention. Again and again, the best literary luck. When I read Maurice I was convinced that Forster had hopelessly distorted the central situation of his novel, because I couldn't believe that a person of 20 or so couldn't know what he wanted sexually. In other words, I thought Forster was avoiding age-of-consent issues by making his characters come to terms with themselves in adulthood. At 14, I couldn't believe that someone 20 or 22 might not know whether or not he loved men.

Well, my beautiful bristle head. I did manage to get a lot of good revision done tonight. Tomorrow, before and after housecleaning on the eve of the arrival of another houseguest, and hopefully sucking off a very handsome prematurely gray married man, yum, for the second time (but that was quite a while ago), must get much more done.

Kevin

--- ▶ ---

FROM: PAUL

DATE: MON, APR 8

Kevin,

Thanks so much for calling me yesterday to tell me about Mormons
on Parade on 60 Minutes. It was touching to think you might be interested in knowing more about my background and culture--in short,
where I'm from. Or maybe you've always been interested in
Mormonism....

   After I spoke to you, I called a buddy and we went for burritos
and margaritas, and then to her house for scotch and Scrabble. I
won, but not by much. Afterward I went to the park, where cruising
was sparse. I got out of my car and walked near the pond, and met
a long-haired Native American fellow who wanted to 69. I though,
what the hell?, so we got mostly naked and sucked one another in
the grass beneath a large tree. He spurted his third load of the
evening into my mouth, and, as per his instructions, I came over his
chest and licked it off. Went home and talked to my roommate until
nearly three a.m.

   Monday, back to school. At noon I headed over to the PE building
men's room and sat on the toilet reading until someone came into
the stall next to mine. The boy was only 23, Chicano and very uncut.
His glans was always hidden in the wrinkled, wet mass of brown
skin that extended beyond the tip of his hard cock. We took turns
sucking on one another, and I enjoyed tasting his plentiful pre-cum-
-creating strings of it that joined my lips to his cock-head. He whispered dirty nothings to me--how he wanted to watch me suck off all
his friends, that he wanted to piss all over me in a public place, that
he wanted to hold me down and watch a series of men gang rape

me. He asked to sniff my underwear, and wanted me to give him the pair I was wearing, but I refused. I simply don't own enough to go around making presents of it to my tricks.

Soon we had company--the librarian guy--and I got on my knees, pulled my T-shirt over my head to avoid soiling it with jiz, and started to suck on his much meatier cock while the kid watched. I was quite proud of the way I was able to keep his thick, lengthy cock in my throat as he grabbed the sides of my stall and pumped his groin into my face, pubic hair grazing my nose and chin with every thrust. I took turns on the two of them until the librarian pulled his cock from my mouth and began to stroke a load out of it. His first spurt created a beautiful and impressive arc in the air before splattering over my eager, open-mouthed face, and I received the remainder of his cum over my face and lips. The kid frantically whispered that he was also about to shoot, so I quickly positioned my head near his cock and received a second shower of jism over my cheeks, my ears, my neck, and mouth. While the cum dripped from my nose and chin and lips, I shot my own load, wishing I had your beautiful face to gaze into as I experienced the sheer ecstasy of cum that only you and I are able to understand.

I headed home and read over 200 pages, watched Jeopardy and The Simpsons (a nightly ritual of mine), made dinner for myself (rosemary chicken with rice and a green salad), and have been working on this damned busy work for the last couple of hours.

All my lovin,

Paul

FROM: KEVIN
DATE: MONDAY NIGHT, APRIL 8
Lord Buddha's birthday
Paul,
Well, my adored fellow, how happy I am to set aside my work to write
to you. I've made a lot of progress today, a surprising amount, but my
publisher is pressing me to finish on time--next Monday, or earlier.

Happily, I was able to squeeze in a pleasurable blowjob this afternoon. Had seen him once before, a long time ago, and was pleased when
he took the bait to come again. 34, very married, very handsome. Tall,
prematurely gray, intelligent face, kind expression, a little sheepish
about being involved in something so depraved. He came today from a
business meeting, so was dressed in a very sexy conservative suit and
tie. As I got most of his clothes off him and sat him down, he said: you
must really love this. I said: hard dick on a handsome guy, what could
be better? Broad-shouldered, big nicely hairy chest, pretty nipples. A
little while later he asked: why do you like this so much? I could only
answer with the usual bemused-butch shake of the head, saying: who
knows? Just love sucking dick, love to be on my knees for a handsome
guy. He was fully hard tout de suite, and appreciative of my ministrations. I loved his cock, only medium-large, but nicely formed, well-
furnished with dark big balls, dark pubic hair in a discreet mass,
against smooth fair skin. Tried to give every possible pleasurable sensation with my mouth and throat. He stroked my head, my back, my
nipples under my T-shirt, so I felt emboldened to take off first my
pants and then my shirt. He pulled on my dick quite a bit, which was
hard the whole time, so hungry was I for his dick. Was he this demon-
strative last time? Can't remember, but think he was decidedly more

reciprocal this time. His questions and comments, too, suggested a curiosity about me, hardened cocksucker, as I am about him, suburban bisexual (or closetcase, or some combination?). For a moment I stood as he stood, let him pull on my dick while I leaned over to suck him. Sucked his nipples, moved into something that was almost an embrace. But soon we were back in our respective positions, I very happy to look up at this sexy suburbanite, he obviously pleased to have me chowing down on his hard-on. He made some moves to hold my head and ears down on his dick, but was too sweet and middle class to be as sexually insistent as I would have liked. Not to complain: I liked his tentativeness, his instinctual reticence, his habit of being gentle, learned no doubt from fucking his wife and girlfriends. With time, perhaps, he'll find that there are times when it's appropriate to hold someone's ears in a vise grip and whale away like a teenager fucking a hole in a watermelon. He let me know he was getting close, and I only escalated, until I felt his hot chloroxy jism at the back of my mouth. Tried to suck every drop out of him, and then jammed my face all the way down to his bush, and let both of us breath and recover. His cock was beautiful afterward, half hard, wet, leaning; a pearl of cum in his pubes that I tried to teeth out. He was just as friendly afterward, laughing a bit at shaking hands at the door.

When you make it back up, I'll propose a three-way with him by e-mail. That's the day's news. Another houseguest tomorrow, and city errands. Will be much distracted, but will be thinking about eating and drinking you.

Kevin

--- ▸ ---

FROM: PAUL

DATE: TUES, APR 9

Kevin,

Once again--you may be logged on at this very moment. Ah serendipity.

My family will be in town over the first weekend of May, so that makes that weekend impossible. Did you say that the weekend of the 27th is difficult as well? If so then either the second or third weekend of May would be fine, although I would be on edge until the dates arrived.

I deposited my tax return so there's nothing I'd rather do than call a travel agent and book a flight to the Bay Area for the near future. Of course, you're still always welcome to come here--most anytime would be great, and you wouldn't need to shoot only for weekends.

Hopefully I can get through this novel today, which means I have no immediate plans for sleaze and sex, but I'll get back to you tonight regardless.

The sun comes up, I think about you,

Paul

--- ▸ ---

FROM: KEVIN

DATE; WEDNESDAY, APRIL 10, 2:30 A.M.

Paul,

Been writing all night, or since eight p.m. anyway. Made lots of progress, closing in on it. Made my way into the city today, met with my editor and then visited an old friend and his boyfriend. They're both pretty wonderful. Elliot is quite ill. Doesn't get out of the house except for doctor's appointments. Spends a lot of his time flat on

his back, takes quite a bit of morphine each day. Was once a cute
blond miniature bodybuilder, is now a frail old man, his face one big
Kaposi's bruise. Thoroughly lovable, still. Lovable, though, like the
other gravely ill people I've had in my life: as a member of another
species, the frail, the in-pain.

Felt not a whit of paradox about going from my tea and sympathy
with them to a booth store on Folsom in search of cock. Found one
immediately, a stocky little blond guy who enthusiastically pumped
my face. Held my head deep against his crotch, pumped his hips in
and out. Then happened on a prince: I peeked into a booth and found
a guy on his knees sucking on the huge dick of a tall slender fair
fellow in his early 20s. Handsome green-eyed face, a little thin in the
lips, real expression in the eyes. When cocksucker left, I peered in
again and asked if I could have a turn. He gave a little guffaw and let
me in. His very hard, very fat dick pointed skyward, my mouth pointed downward. An egalitarian type, he showed a friendly interest in my
body and cock, but I was so captivated by him—not just his beautiful
slender-headed member, but also the way his pubic hair spread in a
delicate fan pattern toward his flat stomach and slender hips by way
of his deep-carved lateral obliques—that I couldn't resist concentrating on sucking him. And he seemed pleased. Rewarded me with a
big splash shot, but he turned away and it hit the wall.

Wasted a good amount of time angling for a shot at a guy or two
who wouldn't buy. Let a good-looking guy suck me through a glory
hole. Regretted not giving big blond dick my number. Then, surprise,
he was back. I sidled up to him and asked how many times a day he
comes. He deflected the question in a friendly way, and invited me to
repeat. Same again, and once again his cum was wasted against the

wall. But this time I gave him my number, and sweetened the deal by saying I was a big deal artiste, that I would be honored to photograph him and suck him off afterward. He seemed receptive and interested, but I doubt very much that he'll call.

I'm wrecked! Getting a carpal tunnel thing from typing. Quarreled with George. Houseguest underfoot for next fortnight——a motor-mouth German lady. I've got my hands full. But I've got you! Though you're sleeping a million miles away. Still, I have you. I have you in my heart, and rejoice in you.

Kevin

--- ▶ ---

FROM: PAUL
DATE: WEDS, APR 10
Kevin,
It's too late; you can't choose not to have a tape, because I'm a good three quarters of the way through it already. I'll send it off soon, but not before I listen to it through a couple of times in the car.

This afternoon I got very horny which made me very distracted which made studying very difficult. So I headed to a nearby Target store where I'd once sucked off a very cute, wiry young man in the restroom. I remember that when he came he became very still, and I could see and feel his cock pulsing between my lips while his cum spurted into my mouth. But alas, no luck today. I did buy a small mirror with which to shave my privates more effectively, a new toothbrush, razor, lip balm, and some blank cassettes. Later, Laura and I went off to Best Buy where I purchased (get ready for this) a VCR! I've decided that a) I simply can't go on without a VCR and b)

I'll never again have a bunch of cash on hand with which to buy one. Unfortunately I have only one porno tape, but it has one of my favorite scenes ever, of a young blond being used and abused by a group of about seven leathermen who make him lick boots, and push anal beads up his ass, and double-dick him in the finale.

I finally jacked off while thumbing through Cum Buddies #1--that photo extravaganza I bought while I was with you nearly 30 days ago. That particular souvenir has gotten a lot of use since I returned from Berkeley.

But now I'm between sleepiness and perverse perkiness because I had a cup of coffee at about seven, and I feel a bit wired even now. I hope you're off having terrific sex with every shape and kind of beautiful man that the Bay Area has to offer. I can see you now, in a white T-shirt, naked from the waist down, squatting on the balls of your feet, your own balls swinging to and fro while you clutch the flexing thighs of a beefy, demanding, mostly straight man who plunges his hard cock in and out of your mouth while cupping the back of your head with his large hands. You deserve the best today and every day.

Alone, but not loaded,
Paul

--- ▸ ---

FROM: PAUL
DATE: WEDS, APR 10
Kevin,
So I couldn't wait any longer to arrange to visit that incredibly handsome man in the photo I received today, so I called

Southwest and made reservations. I'll arrive in Oakland at 12:55 p.m. Thursday the 16th and leave 5:30 p.m. Sunday afternoon. Is that acceptable? I'm glad I made the plans today, because the fares go up after 10 p.m. tonight.

Now I'll be on pins and needles until May 16th, but just know that if for any reason you are able to make your way this direction before then, you are more than welcome to stay with me. (I'll be extending the invitation until I make myself a perfect pest, I'm sure.)

I've got to get on to class. As always it was sensational to talk to you, if only for a few minutes, and I hope your book introduction is materializing as you'd like. I'm sure it will be terrific.

Take care, my Roman god, and I'll write soon.

Paul

--- ▶ ---

FROM: KEVIN
DATE: LATE WEDNESDAY, APRIL 10

Paul,

So glad to hear your voice, thanks for calling. Very glad you'll be coming up, hope arrangements go well. I finished the book today, hurrah. It even seems to be in fairly good shape, considering how knocked-together it was at the end.

Cranky, though. George and I continue to quarrel, about minis-cule things and huge things. Our houseguest, however charming and lilting her accent, is an exasperating conversational steamroller. Two weeks of this.

I'm being boycotted in my sex ads. Think I've perhaps exhausted the pool of AOL and print-personal men who need cocksucking.

Seems hardly credible, I know, especially since I make myself sound irresistible, but no one responds. Thanks for making me a tape, I know I'll love it. I have porno tapes for you, lots of schlock, but some good ones. Congrats on the VCR purchase, a necessity after all. Lots of print porn for you too. Amazing how we both look for the same stuff--cum shots in an open mouth, for one thing. I think you go more for the slightly sleazy-looking guys being sleazy, while I like choir boys being sleazy, so lucky for us that I'm rather seedy and you're downright altar-boyish--though less so no doubt, after your buzz cut.

Much love,

Kevin

--- ▸ ---

FROM: PAUL
DATE: THURS, APR 11
Kevin,

Sorry to hear about your exasperation with houseguests and quarrels, though I'm glad to hear you finished the book--congratulations! Wish I were there to give you a well-deserved back and shoulder rub, although in reality I'm terrible with massages. Maybe I could give you a well-deserved lick-down instead.

I'm so tempted to head off to Blue Cut this morning/afternoon, but I really need to get back into my reading. I keep trying to fool myself that I could take it along and get reading done between blowjobs, but this never happens. Then again, I'd also like to get more sun on my face. I could take a towel, a backpack, and set up camp, reading Clarissa as passers-by come over to me for dick action. Have I convinced myself yet?

Last night I went to a birthday party for Max, and flirted (finally) with a lanky, beautiful dancer I've had a crush on for months. He seemed receptive, and even dropped a couple of sleazy double-entendres himself. When I got up to go piss, I said, "God, I have to pee which means I have to get up." And he responded with "You wouldn't have to get up if you had a good enough friend to help you out." Hmmm. I certainly wouldn't mind having sex with him. I'll keep you posted.

Your tape is finished, and I listened to it in the car yesterday and today. It ended up being a little more sappy and chock-full of love songs than I'd planned, but I guess that was inevitable.

I'll check on you tonight. Hope your day is relaxing and sexually productive.

Take care,
Paul

--- ▶ ---

FROM: KEVIN
DATE: LATE THURSDAY, APRIL 11
Paul,

A clamorous day. Attended the queer-lit talk on campus. Enjoyed it thoroughly. The talk took place in a comfortable English department lounge on the third floor of Wheeler hall, sunlight pouring in. The noises of spring sometimes intruded from outside, so conscientious grad students closed the windows. Thoroughly enjoyed a bit of vicarious access to Dryden et al, a culture I barely know. Enjoyed your prof.'s friendly, direct manner, appreciated that another small blow was being struck for truth and queerdom. Enjoyed being privy to a rarefied academic experience. Was charmed by him, obviously a very good person, and accosted him shamelessly, talked about how I knew about him through you. So it turns out that yes, as I suspected, everybody I know knows everybody you know. We talked about how wonderful you are, me looking down and reddening, I'm certain, visibly. It is a very small world.

So at least I had some tenuous connection with you, attending the talk of your professor and friend, seeing him again later at the museum. There is an appeal to conducting our affair in the vacuum of two-boys-adrift-on-an-anonymous-ocean-of-sex, and there is an attraction to realizing that there are all sorts of unexpected connections between us, and we are in fact involved in a romance surrounded by intersecting webs of friendship and acquaintanceship. Even in the late twentieth century there is an amusing potential for scandal. I must say that I am so proud of being associated with you that I can't worry about any complications at all. For you I would be proud to undergo any, any humiliation. I almost crave it. I would like to undertake extreme activities on your behalf, kidnap and rape Republicans, I don't know what, but something fittingly outrageous. Anyway, for now, nothing more extreme than polite introductions have been exchanged. But another bridge has been crossed. In a characteristic Bay Area way, it turns out that everyone we know is an ex-boyfriend of everyone else we know. We no longer belong to each other in a hermetic cybersex way, no one knowing but us. Hope you don't mind. I love you so much I would like to suck your cock in Sproul Plaza at noon, for the delectation of the crowd, even of the loony Christian missionaries.

I don't think I can wait five weeks to see you. In the meantime
know that I love you.

Kevin

--- ▶ ---

FROM: PAUL

DATE: FRI, APR 12

Kevin,

I just got back from lunch and coffee with my prof. and he gave me
the book you sent with him. I don't deserve the showers of attention I
receive from you. He said he enjoyed you very much and was pleased
to have you in the audience and to get to know you better afterward.

Of course I was able to talk myself into going to Blue Cut this afternoon, Last night I heard someone refer to it as Cocksucker Canyon.

First Ron and I went to have coffee and read. I absorbed myself
in Clarissa and Ron read Ginsburg. He read the raunchier poems
aloud to me. Then I went to our local occult/metaphysical boutique,
where I looked for Rachel Pollack's Seventy-Eight Degrees, but they
weren't around. Only her stuff on the Haindl Tarot.

Then I was off to Blue Cut, your cassette blaring away in my
deck. The afternoon was slow, and I spent over three hours there;
needless to say I read very little. I did suck on a very attractive red-
head with a winning smile and a gorgeous, intense stare. I must
have worked on his nicely shaped and sized cock for nearly an hour,
running my tongue along the veins, placing the tip of my tongue in
his piss-slit, sucking on both his balls at once, etc, but he never
came. He also never took his eyes off me, and I found the whole
experience extraordinarily sexy. By the time he said he had to get on

home, I was nearly paralyzed from remaining on my knees so long.

Next I followed a cruising idiot around for far too long while he stared at the sky, the mountains, the freeway, and then repositioned himself a few more yards away from me. This was maddening, and I finally gave up on him.

Walking back toward my car, I ran across a mechanic with his name embroidered on a patch on his shirt. I sucked on his miniscule dick for a while, until he began to whimper and plead "Please d on't hurt me." I told him I had to be somewhere, but he really wanted to come, so I told him to be quick about it. Took his load on my face, and went to the stream to wash up.

Next was a cute Hispanic boy walking around in a pair of Levi shorts with the fly unzippped and wrenched open. He was very aggressive about fucking my face, and produced a prodigious amount of pre-cum. I spent a good deal of time creating frail, sticky strands of it stretching from his cock head to my lips or tongue. When he finally got ready to cum, he pulled his cock out to jack himself off, and shot his load into my opened mouth. He enjoyed looking at the pool of cum on my tongue, and I took his cock back in my mouth and allowed it to soften completely before I let him leave.

My last adventure was perhaps the most successful. Two men-- one black and sexy and bald, the other a bit hick-like, pudgy, and white--were cruising one another as I joined the ritual and made it clear that I would suck them both. The bald guy immediately doused his penis in lotion and told me he wasn't interested in being sucked, but that he'd like to watch me suck the other. I obliged him, and sucked on the baseball-capped hick forever while baldy muttered "Yeah suck him, take his cum." When the hick began to spurt, I took his load all over my face, and immediately had to turn the other cheek for baldy's load. Then, with a huge, thick strand of cum literally pouring off my lower lip, I stood and shot my own load into the trees. Wish I had a photo of myself, cum dripping off my face as I shot into the air.

Later, I got a call from a guy I met a while back in LA and we had phone sex. So I got plenty of orgasms in, but not enough reading. Isn't that just how it goes? If only we were graded and paid for the amount and quality of orgasms we produced.

I think I'll crash a little earlier than usual tonight. I think I may have a cold coming on, and I want to get rid of it right away.

I love you,

Paul

--- ▶ ---

FROM: PAUL

DATE: SATURDAY, APRIL 13

Kevin,

I spent the morning with Maria, drinking coffee and walking through an open-air market downtown. I bought two pairs of sunglasses and a box of otter pops. Came home and cleaned my room, ate salad and read for a couple of hours. Why the compulsion to give you the details of my days?

My encounter with the lunatic mechanic yesterday made me remember another lusty lunatic I met while at school. I was a first year student and had just found the cruising spots on BYU's campus. While in one of the restrooms at the student union center, I ran into a harmless looking but not terribly handsome fellow who wanted to take me to his apartment which, he assured me, was not far from campus. I had avoided going to people's houses thus far, but for some reason I was up for an adventure. His apartment was very far away though, and we had very little to say as we walked there. Once in his bedroom, I was a little disconcerted to see large reproduction of Jesus Christ hanging over his bed, with photos of various Mormon elders and temples adorning the walls. We took our clothes off and got into bed where, if I remember correctly, I 69ed with someone for the first time. He began to get a bit romantic with me, telling me he wanted to take me to Switzerland--where he'd served his Mormon mission. He produced a Toblerone candy bar, gave me a bite, and lovingly said, "This is the kind of candy they eat there." I wa s getting nervous at this point, but he begged me to stay and fuck him. I had never fucked anyone before, so I decided to take advantage of the opportunity. He put lotion on my dick, and slid himself onto me while I lay on my back on his bed. After he had been sliding up and down on my throbbing cock for only a few minutes, I warned him I was about to cum. He looked me in the eyes, and told me he wanted me to cum inside him. As he slid back down on my dick, I exploded in him, and he ecstatically collapsed onto my chest.

"Now we're married," he muttered. "You're inside me for eternity, and we'll be man and wife for ever and ever." This was too much for me, so I wriggled out from under him, washed myself at his sink, and began to get dressed. He whimpered and sobbed after me, begging me to stay and hold him, that we were married now so I couldn't leave. I told him I had a class, but that maybe I could I drop by later. Somehow I pacified him, and got the hell away. While I was cleaning up and dressing, however, I kept eyeing him--fully expecting he was going to reach beneath his bed and produce an ax or chainsaw or electric drill....

The risks we take as cruisers.

I'll miss you tonight, and won't be able to retrieve my mail until tomorrow, late. I'll certainly be on edge until then. I hope your weekend is going well. I adore you and wish you were my bedmate tonight.

Paul

--- ▶ ---

FROM: PAUL
DATE: SUN, APR 14
Kevin,

You are the sweetest most delectable thing alive. I perfectly swooned after our conversation the other night, you made me useless for my guests, who were actually getting on just fine without me. I was soaring miles above the earth.

Yes, the peacemaker role is one that gets me into trouble. "You're so nice" is the pathetic little phrase that acquaintanc es use most to describe me. I can't bear confrontation or hurt feelings, and will do absolutely anything at nearly any cost to myself to avoid such problems. Even now, I've met a terrific bunch of fags and dykes here at school, and I can't bear the fact that occurrences prior to my arrival have caused rifts among my new-found friends. I've spent a lot a lot of the last few months trying to get all my friends to like one another, and it's actually working. Of course, as you've mentioned, such a drive for peace and harmony can often make us miserable and martyred.

After dinner, I went to the opening of a new coffee shop that is

stunningly inappropriate for this very drab, very suburban community. The shop is gay-owned and absolutely gorgeous with something
like 25'high copper paneled ceilings and wonderful parlor furniture.
It also drew a great crowd of future patrons--from as far away as
Laguna Beach, no less!

I was talking with friends when I spotted my crush from the dance
department, Aaron. He was with an incredibly annoying guy, but we
were flirting unabashedly when a very burly Schwarzenegger-type
wandered up and began to talk dirty with all of us. We all moved over
to the bar next to the coffee shop--one of our two gay bars--and the
newcomer (Alex) and I drank far too much beer and had nothing short
of incredibly sexy foreplay at the bar for over two hours. Aaron was a
very enthusiastic spectator, and at first I felt badly for having been
sucked into the attentions of Alex when I'd originally had my sights on
Aaron, but he seemed very willing to watch me enjoy myself and
wasn't the least bit put off by my decision to take Schwarzenegger
home with me. This is the first time I've taken anyone home since I
moved here, a big step, but he was nasty and muscle-bound, and
was wearing an impressive metal cock ring, so I couldn't resist.

At home, we made out, and he made me lick his boots. I sucked
his cock, rimmed his clean but musky asshole, and buried my nose
and tongue in his gloriously smelly armpits.

Then he announced that he needed to pee, and he told me to get
in the shower so he could piss all over me--heaven! He was
impressed that I would take his urine in my mouth and swallow it--it
was actually the tastiest piss I'd ever experienced, and he doused
me from head to toe. Next he fucked me mercilessly while calling
me all sorts of nasty things and spitting in my face. I was at my pig-

boy-bottom-best and enjoying every minute of it. We culminated the scene with my coming on his chest, and his straddling my chest with his trunk-like thighs and spurting his cum onto my mouth and chin, while I licked it from my lips.

Like a stereotypical straight male, he collapsed, demanded a blanket, and started to snore before I'd so much as closed my eyes. I had a miserable night's sleep, but every so often he'd shove his fingers into my mouth and probe it while pushing his erection up against my ass-crack. This morning he mounted me and rubbed himself up against my belly until he shot a load. I was a little disappointed that our morning sex was so much more conventional than that of the night before, but I suppose we can't have everything we want. I also awoke with a frightful sunburn. I had spent the entire day with Clarissa next to the pool at friends', and had no idea how baked I was getting.

So today I'm going to call Aaron and give him the dripping details--I'm sure he'll be beside himself with envy. I really think he wanted a three-way, but it was quite clear that Alex didn't want to tackle us both. I think Aaron will end up being a nice partner in crime for me, and I certainly wouldn't mind having three-ways with him if we went hunting for sleazy tops together.

So even after two cups of coffee, I'm still pretty groggy. (Alex actually looked at me this morning after his solo orgasm and said, "So why don't you put some coffee on, OK?" Just brutal. I love it.) Gotta get perky and deal with Clarissa again. I got nearly 200 pages read yesterday, but need to get at least that much read today.

I miss you and wish you were with me this morning. I'd love to blow off all my plans and demands to have a continuous sex-fest with you, from which I wouldn't emerge until tomorrow morning outside my prof.'s office. Take care, and know I love you more than ever.

Paul

--- ▲ ---

FROM: KEVIN

DATE: MONDAY, APRIL 15, 5:00 P.M.

Paul,

Was told today that book is way too long, had been difficult to judge length with so many illustrations, so spent a few hours slashing and rearranging. Went well, easier to make the cuts than I would have thought.

Went to the baths last night, as I said on the phone I might. Your experience with muscleboy Alex inspired me. I came home though too tired to write you then. Felt like I'd let us down, not committing it all directly to text. And it is a bit of a fog today, perhaps because the sex wasn't all that wonderful. Must have sucked ten cocks or so. Some only wanted to be sucked for a short while, others I didn't want to continue sucking after a short while. The most involved contact was with the first, a handsome 36-year-old bodybuilder, medium height, rockhard butt. He enjoyed being sucked, though he didn't get very hard. Leaned down to invite me to join him in a sprawl on the mats in the next room. There he vouchsafed that he was much hung-up about not being harder, did I mind? Reassured him, kissed a lot, then resumed mouthing him. He leaned over to engage in some 69 stuff. My hard dick looked nice in his wholesome-looking face. Before long he jacked himself to climax, refusing me his load. Exchanged friendly words, a last kiss.

A sweet-faced, blond, bulky (but not fat), mid-30s guy, wearing
wire-rims and a conspiratorial smile, stuck his fairly enormous dick
in my face several times. A pair of 20-something beauties, former
frat boys, let me suck them both for a while. A scruffy 40-year old—
glasses, beard—waved his dick at me several times before I deigned
to take the beautiful long thing down my throat. Ran my hands over
his lithe and astonishingly well-muscled body. He had let several others suck him before me, but he seemed to be working toward shooting. Pleased as always, even so I was deciding that I didn't particularly
want his load when he silently filled my throat with warm cum and
my mouth with the taste of him. What the hell. Loved the taste, finished him off, saluted him with a pat on the thigh and a thank you. I
love to thank guys after I suck them off. Takes them off guard.
They're physically drained, I've done all the work—they think, usually,
that they should be thanking me. I like though the unexpected cour-
tesy, the reminder to myself that I'm grateful to be sucking cock.

So those are the high points. Many dreary moments of waiting
and wandering. Many men disdained me. Ran into one slight acquaintance early in the evening. Ignored each other, though I tried to nod
an avowal. Then a friendly acquaintance, a friendly artist, crossed
my path. We exchanged friendly, fleet hellos. But when a real buddy
turned up, a friend who thinks of me as a married person (I am
after all), and who thinks of himself as a man of refinement and
education (he is after all), then I decided it was time to go home. It
was clear we'd get in each other's way. We've run into each other
there before. This time he looked straight at me without acknowl-
edgment. As a philanderer, I'm the one who ought to feel any awkwardness, but it's not easy to relax in the pursuit of anonymous sex

in the presence of erstwhile dinner companions.

All evening I felt what a second-rate experience the whole thing was, how much better it would be if you were there.

Love,

Kevin

--- ▸ ---

FROM: KEVIN

DATE: MONDAY, APRIL 15, 11:30 P.M.

Paul,

Just returned from seeing a romantic movie with houseguest and friends, and, while cynically weighing tropes of direction, editing, and sound track, thought about my own "great love", how much I love him, and how beautiful he is. I thought about how much I love his frame, slender and strong as a young tree. I see him leaning over me during sex, unutterably sexy.

I linger in memory over your extraordinary eyes, green and blue and gray, and remember how shy I was about gazing into them too long. My hands remember the feel of your skin, your body's corners and contours, the wonderful line and mass of you. The special color of your skin, a burnished gold. The ripple of the delicate hairs of your legs and the crack of your ass, rippling under my hands. I remember the taste and firmness of your dick in my mouth—is there anything more perfect? I see your head inclined in your pho-tograph, your shy irresistible smile, and think how foolish it is to be in love with you after seeing you so briefly. But I am in love with you, and proud of you for being so beautiful, humble about your returning these sentiments, worried about your being eventually

disappointed in me, confidant that whatever happens I have been
lucky to know you and to feel about you as I do, certain that whatever happens I will always, always revere you.

    Kevin

--- ▶ ---

FROM: KEVIN
DATE: WEDNESDAY AFTERNOON, APRIL 17
Paul,

Thanks for your phone message this morning, sorry I missed you.
I'm guessing that your e-mail is down. Hope all is well.

    Talked to the magazine buyer for A Different Light SF yesterday,
to ask him about the store's parameters as far as
indecency/obscenity are concerned. He was friendly and inclusive,
saying he would have trouble with something racist, but that he and
the store were most sex-positive. I pressed him, wondering if Drunk
On Cum (DOC for short), would be a problem, or a spurting dick on
the cover. He said they didn't believe in censorship, and supported
sluttishness. So what do you think? Any titles for our true-life long
distance romance occur to you? The other night my dreams were
filled with paste-up strategies and schemes. Isn't it just like a fag,
to work through design issues in his sleep? Perhaps because I've
just finished my latest manuscript, I'm casting about for a project.
Must say that I've become intrigued by the idea of publishing our
correspondence, changing only what we must to protect the guilty.
Amazing too that you had the same idea all along, and both of us
almost from the beginning. The idea of publishing our dirty letters
has prompted me to be completely honest, to reveal myself utterly,

and yet to stand back to see how this might read for a third party.
Of course I'm too close to have any perspective, but I think it might
amuse people. Besides, a certain number of boys in SF or LA who
thumbed through these pages might legitimately expect to find
themselves described in our roman à clef, roman à bite.

No sex yesterday, but Jason, actor/erotic performer from the
Campus Theater, came, at my invitation, to pose for my photo group.
He was a hit. In the bright light of the studio he was even sexier
than in the dim lights of the porn joint. He has a slender-but-volup-
tuous build, right from a Pontormo drawing: graceful head, long
neck, wonderful arms and chest, bubble butt, muscular well turned
legs. Big soft convex peach-colored nipples. Distracting to photograph him, because his nipples cried out not to be recorded, but
chewed, as his butt begged to be tongued, and his handsome dick
deserved lots of loving attention. The latter was, in repose, longish,
cut, clustered with big balls in a rather abundant light chestnut
patch. I was secretly relieved that he didn't scare the horses by getting erect, and doubly relieved that, for all my yearning to eat him
up, I had already had the privilege several times of having him jam
his big dick down my throat, with others watching, at the theater.

Just surprised with call and visit from John H, the pretty, too-
tanned blond boy with the monster dong whom I sucked off--twice--
at the dirty bookstore last week. He even drove across the bridge for
my ministrations. Was as cute as ever, nervous, friendly-polite. I gave
him a glass of water and drew him up to the light-filled bedroom,
where he stripped at my suggestion. Showed him some of my photos,
said (again) that I would like to shoot him. But his cock was already
hard and bobbing when his pants came off, and I couldn't resist

throwing myself onto my knees to get his dick in my mouth immediately. 20 minutes then of happy sucking in various positions, straining somewhat to get to the best--his dick starts immensely fat at the root and tapers to a smaller head. Sucked his big balls, moved down his perineum to his almost hairless asshole to tongue fuck him. Quiet throughout, this and the rest he nonetheless enjoyed, and he rolled onto his belly to let me eat him with a round buttock in each hand, pulling his gold cheeks apart to see the wet puckered sphincter twitching for the return of my tongue. He turned onto his back and came on his belly while I was sucking his big scrotum. I was a touch disappointed, I really wanted to drink his cum this time, but I contented myself with licking some of it off the dark blond hairs of his belly and sucking the last drops out of his still-stiff dick. That was fun, he said, satisfied and sheepish, and quickly dressed. Who knows if he'll call again. How I'd love to work on him with you, together.

Now I feel shy about sending this to you immediately, in case your e-mail problem includes messages like this going astray, or being read by the computer-doctor over your shoulder. Paranoid, perhaps, but I'll hold off sending this until tonight, by which time I may have spoken to you.

Kevin

--- ▶ ---

FROM: KEVIN
DATE: WEDNESDAY, APRIL 17, AFTER 11:00 P.M.
Paul,
So I admit I feel deprived of you, though I loved hearing your voice today. Thanks for calling back. Thought I'd have another assignation

tonight, but just as well that it fell through. Will sign off and send this on to you, even if you won't see it for a while, or it will have to be re-sent. Last message received from you was Sunday afternoon. Tempted to call again. Congratulations for getting over the hump with Clarissa.

Since we'll be taking pseudonyms for our own epistolary novel, how about taking the names Lyle and Eric Menendez? The boys were sentenced today to life in prison. Has a nice, dirty, Leopold-and-Loeb quality. Besides, would have to figure out again which one is the cute one (would have to be portrayed by you), and which one is the homo and LIKES toothbrushes stuck up his bum (we'll arm wrestle).

God I miss you. Staring blankly at the blinking cursor on the screen, trying to think how to say how much I long for you.

Kevin

--- ▶ ---

FROM: PAUL
DATE: THURS, APRIL 18
Kevin,
All I have are paltry and insufficient thanks to you for being available to me last night. Although I wasn't necessarily traumatized over the affair, I was so relieved to have someone I hold so dear at the receiving end of my story, understanding. If only I could have held you closer, but the soothing tones of your voice through an inadequate receiver was more comforting than you can imagine. I can't think what I could ever have done to become worthy of you.

Last night, after my evening seminar, I joined friends to watch a movie and have dinner. We drank some wine, ate pizza, and enjoyed

>d.o.c.

watching all the stereotypes of Staten Island working girls wasted
on our very German friend Bernd. I left them at about midnight, and
since they live close to the park, I decided I would drive by to see
who might be around before I went home. It was a cold, misty
evening, and the park looked fairly empty. There was one car parked
beneath a street lamp near the lake, so I decided I would walk along
a path there before circling the park and heading home. The car
belonged to an older gentleman who was wrapped in blankets and
fishing, but I decided I would continue down the path along the lake
anyway. Now I remember that there was no moon.

As I entered into a darker area of the park, I noticed six figures
walking toward me, so I immediately made a 45 degree turn toward
a patch of light mere yards away, and they followed me asking me
for a light and then demanding to know what I was doing in the park
so late. I refused to even turn around as I quickly walked toward a
street where an old brown pickup had just parked along the curb. I
asked the owner of the truck, who had seen me and my pursuers, if
he might give me a ride to my car. He seemed hesitant, but could
tell I was in trouble, so he jumped back into his truck, and I ran to
the passenger's side and hopped in, while the six men began to yell
toward us "fucking faggots."

Since my car was still too near for me to feel absolutely safe, I
asked him to keep driving around the park so that the punks wouldn't
see where I was parked. We drove about a third of the way around
the park's lake and parked beneath a street lamp. My rescuer was a
good-looking man, probably in his 50s, with a moustache and a
very working-class demeanor. He unzipped his pants and pulled out
a nice-sized hard-on which I of course began to suck while he

groaned and stretched out in his seat and placed his hands behind my head.

Not five minutes had passed, however, before he noticed the same bunch of young men coming up on my side of the car, so he bolted upright, locked his door and I locked mine. The boys began to hit my side of the truck with their fists, smacking the window as though they meant to break it. Meanwhile, the man who told me his name was Jess, tried to start the engine, but his truck simply wouldn't start. We each had three boys on either side of us, hammering the truck, but soon one of the bashers on my side had found a wheel rim somewhere, and was swinging it at the window. They were trying to break into the truck and we needed to get out. Jess opened his door and we both leaped out the driver's side, and ran in different directions down the street.

I was sprinting as fast as I could, while at least three of the thugs followed at my heels. A blue pickup drove near me, and the driver began to slow down to a speed that would allow me to jump into the bed of his truck. I vaulted in and he sped me back to my car further down the road. I jumped out and told him to call the police, got into my own car and raced back to Jess's truck.

Jess had somehow gotten back into his truck and his group of bashers had used the tire rim to break through his door window; they were trying to pull him from the car through the window. I leaned on my horn, flashed my lights and began to spin my car in circles around the six men. Some of them began to chase me, pounding on my car as I passed and twice they tried to hit my car with the tire rim. When they got too close I would race ahead and then turn and come back to begin my distractions anew. Jess mean-

while couldn't get close enough to the passenger side of my car to
get in and away from his attackers.

Finally I saw the attackers flee to another side of the park, so I
began to search for Jess, but couldn't find him. I looked in the cab
of his truck: nothing but shattered glass. I panicked and raced
toward a phone booth on the other side of the lake, nearly colliding
with other drivers as I made my way. The phone was being used by
someone with a silver truck, so I jumped out of the car and shouted
that I needed to call the police because someone had been badly
beaten. The driver was already talking to 911 and asked for an ambu-
lance. I returned to where Jess had been parked, but he had
returned and driven away. I could see his truck in the distance frantically veering out of the park. Later I would find out that he had
been hiding under his truck when I couldn't find him.

I raced after and caught up with him about two miles from the
park. I motioned for him to pull over, I went to him to see how badly
he was hurt. He was short of breath and could not speak a few
moments, but then he was able to tell me that he'd been kicked
badly. He also had blood on his shoulder, and he told me that one
boy was using a knife. Jess refused to go to the hospital, even
though one was nearby, because he had no insurance and was
unemployed. When he tried to get out of his truck, he nearly collapsed. I told him we needed to call the police, but he panicked at
that suggestion as well. Finally I convinced him to give me his
boyfriend's number; they'd had an argument earlier in the evening. I
called his friend and told him where Jess was, that he'd been beat-
en and hurt, but that he refused to go to the hospital or to the
police. Meanwhile, Jess shouted to me to tell Marcos that he loved

him and he wasn't doing anything in the park.

 After Marcos came to drive Jess home, I went back to the park
to find the police and make a report. When I got there I saw the six
boys handcuffed and squatting on the ground, and the police
immediately asked me what I wanted there. They seemed reluctant
to take my statement, but I insisted, and told my story to an officer who seemed distracted and put out at having to listen to my
account. He made me repeat details again and again, and then
asked a junior officer to come over and take my report. So I began
my tale all over again, while the new officer asked for the same
details over and over. They seemed unconvinced that a tire rim
could be used as a weapon, despite the fact that the attackers
had used it to break into the truck and to threaten us. They told me
that nothing I'd seen or experienced amounted to enough evidence
to detain these youths any longer, and that only Jess' testimony
would be sufficient to have them arrested. One of the kids had a
warrant out for his arrest, so he was taken to jail, but I passed
the other five as I drove out of the park, wondering who the real
bashers were.

 Whereas I could somehow place these punks in a social context
that would, if not justify, at least partially explain their behavior
that evening, I was at a loss how to deal with the police and their
absolute indifference and lack of concern. One officer told me that
as soon as I had been driven back to my own car, I should have
gone home. He never even said I should have called the police along
the way, or once I'd arrived home. I was furious that he thought so
little of someone's life that he could insinuate that calling the police
was an unnecessary step. At least three of us park-cruising fags

called the police that night, and I'm actually proud that I belong to a (sub) community that is willing to risk police harassment and ridicule to help save another member of the community whose life was in danger. I've always romanticized the cruising community somewhat, but this small manifestation of solidarity was a nice indicator that some of these fantasies I entertain may be true.

This account of a quite maddening and frightening Wednesday night would not be complete, however, if I were not to mention the most soothing experience of calling you, Kevin, and having you listen, carefully and caringly, to every detail of my narrative. Speaking with you was the perfect palliative for my jumpy nerves and frazzled mind, and I was once again reminded of how lucky I am to have met a boy named Kevin in Berkeley.

--- ▶ ---

FROM KEVIN
DATE: FRIDAY, APRIL 19
Paul,
Still shocked by your ordeal last night, grateful that you were unhurt, proud of you for doing the right thing at every scary step. Instinct, that. You scarcely had the opportunity to second-guess yourself. It was so hard to hear the stress in your voice and not be able to help. I'm so glad you called me, so glad I was just awake enough to pick up the phone. I hate to think you might have gotten the machine. In thought I am always caressing you, kissing you, clutching you to me, pressing as much of you against me as I can, intertwining toes. Last night, hearing your harrowing story, I wanted all that and to comfort you too. Then I eroticize comforting you, and

imagine lightly kissing your closed eyes, stroking your head against my heart, soothing you with a long stroking touch, like a groom with a skittish colt.

   Kevin

--- --- ---

FROM PAUL
DATE: SAT, APR 20
Kevin,
I feel so awful that I haven't had the time to be at my computer and writing to you on the regular basis I'm used to. Somehow the universe conspired against me all week, and I haven't had time to do anything I really want.

   To catch you up on the more juicy details of the week's events:

   Tuesday I traveled up to Blue Cut Canyon after a meeting and spent far too much time for far too little. I was also dressed in shorts and a T-shirt, so that when it got overcast and began to rain, I was very unprepared but still loath to leave (my relentless libido).

   I did run into a very attractive guy named Eddie who had a very long and thin penis, which never got fully hard. He wanted an audience for my sucking performance and I spent a good hour following him around the canyon looking for promising onlookers to no avail. We had a nice conversation despite his promiscuous use of the word "Oriental" to describe Asian men (which he categorically dismissed from his erotic economy). Finally I needed to get back to attend a boring dinner party, and so I left the canyon to get home, wash, and dress just in time for dinner.

   Afterward, I recalled how pent-up I was, so I drove through the

park and very quickly sucked a beautiful large uncut cock to comple-
tion--enormous gush of cum into my mouth and throat with just the
right amount of heaving and thrusting. Meanwhile, a beautiful black
dancer who'd been watching and produced an even larger cock for me
to work on. It was severely curved downward which made sucking
the entire dick impossible, but he enjoyed my ministrations regardless. When he got ready to cum, I pulled my mouth off his cock and
positioned it inches away from his swollen glans. Soon he was direct-
ing his massive load into my eager maw, and he refused to go soft. I
sucked on him again, but he was nervous about what were possibly
police cars circling the park, so we went to a spot near a bridge that
crosses the Santa Ana, and I spent another hour sucking on his gorgeous cock and was rewarded with another tasty load of his jism.

You'll probably think me insane, but I went to the park again
Thursday night--mostly because I wanted to defy bashers, police
and the park itself by proving I was more in control of my nocturnal
affairs than I'd begun to feel. The evening began with a dinner date
with Aaron, the dancer, and we had a nice pasta meal and wine.
Afterward, we parked at a spot near the one by the river I mentioned
before. We made out in the car and then took a short walk to a place
where we explored each other's upper bodies and faces, but
refrained from even unbuttoning our jeans. He wanted to go home
fairly early, and although I was having a fine time, I was also happy
to drop him off--I suspect he's seeing someone else, though I don't
mind. He's sweet, beautiful, and a wild kisser, but somehow he
doesn't succeed in capturing all my attentions.

So I dropped him off at his apartment which is very near the
park, and then drove to the park where I immediately met a very

burly, growling bearded fellow who loved to chew on my tits and have me suck on his cock. I even persuaded him to drain a load of piss into my mouth when he went soft. He never came, despite the inclusion of three different men--one of whom I happily sucked to completion. The evening was reassuring and the large number of cruising men gave the park a sense of safety and community that had been threatened by the proceedings of the night before.

And I'm missing you as usual, although you've been terrific about keeping me well supplied with gorgeous love-letters. No one has ever made me feel about myself the way you do. But my planned visit to you is now less than a month away, and I can hardly wait to see you, although I'm also feeling a bit of trepidation. I so terribly want not to disappoint you, and then I feel I'm merely being presumptuous. But I've fallen for you, and want badly to have your flesh beneath my fingertips, between my lips and teeth, before my eyes.

I hope your weekend was wonderful, and am looking forward to a more consistent communication this upcoming week.

As always I love you,

Paul

--- ▶ ---

FROM PAUL
DATE: TUES, APR 23
Kevin,
I couldn't wait to write and tell you how happy I was to hear your voice and learn about your latest, most romantic scheme. I feel especially undeserving of you now, and am thinking about all the ways that I fail to successfully return your endearing gestures of

affection. I'm still quite aware that I haven't mailed you your cassette, even though I've listened to it a number of times already. Am
I worried what you'll think of my taste? And after all, it is a bit of an
adolescent thing to do. Certainly nothing as meaningful as a signed
book. After I hung up today, I realized that I tend to jabber away on
the phone, monopolizing the conversations with triteness and stam-
mers, and I wondered if I come across as more bitchy than I truly
am I hope not. I question the way I seem to mismanage my time and
money so that I cause you to be (inexplicably) hungry for more of my
messages. Please don't take this as a lure for pity--I know you are
capable of the deepest sort of empathy and affection I've ever
encountered in a person--but I only want to accuse myself, a little,
of some very real foibles that are unwarranted obstacles in my loving you the way I wish. And we certainly have obstacles enough as
it is. Now I'm feeling conspicuously confessional.

My friend Aaron--the guy I went to dinner with on Thursday--called
today and asked, quite boldly, if I might be interested in pursuing a
dating relationship. I told him I enjoyed his company very much, that
I'd had a good time Thursday night, and that I'd love to spend more
time with him in a kind of "romantic friendship" (a good old ei gh-
teenth-century concept). We then proceeded to warn one another of
our respective limitations. He's getting over a bout with a particularly
nasty STD and is only barely beginning to develop his "top tend en-
cies." For my part I told him I was deeply involved emotionally with a
man in Berkeley with whom I correspond and who I planned to visit in
May, that I was not interested in our dating each other exclusively,
and that I was HIV-positive. He had no problem with any of the above,
and all that was lacking was a proper shake of hands. He told me he

thought I was a nice "affectionate buddy"--a term I liked much better than "romantic friendship," since it had a more casual ring to it--and we decided to hang out this coming Friday night.

It was such a strange conversation in that we both felt absolutely confident in sorting through the messier, business-like details a relationship inevitably brings, and we seemed quite in agreement about the noncommittal nature of our desires to "hang out" together. Then again, there was a perfunctory quality to the whole conversation, as well. Honesty can require a certain bluntness I suppose. I still don't know how, exactly, I feel about Aaron. The best of all possible worlds would have allowed you and me to be closer to each other, at least physically, in some way, and if we never became lovers in any conventional sense, we would be....I can't think quite how to end that sentence, because I can't possibly wish for anything more. (Actually, I yearn and ache to have you so close that you roam beneath my skin.) I love all the non-traditional aspects of our romance--our desire to hear and encourage each other's sexual exploits, the scandalous, yet very mannered and measured quality of our affair, the reassuring, yet arousing, affection that streams from you to me in a tempo that somehow echoes the frequency with which your much-missed cock spurts much-desired loads of cum. You both penetrate and consume me in ways I've never experienced before, and I'm absolutely addicted to you.

I love you and am so eager to feel you under my fingertips again.

Wet dreams,

Paul

--- ▶ ---

>d.o.c.

FROM KEVIN

DATE: WEDNESDAY, APRIL 24

Paul,

Your worries are totally unfounded, though they only endear you to
me more, as everything about you increases my love for you. There
is nothing undeserving about you in any way, especially as concerns
me. Please don't be hard on yourself. I love you so much, don't want
to imagine that you are worrying unduly. You'll see soon that I don't
deserve the high place you give me, there is no reason to place me
in any way above you (except physically, occasionally), that the only
thing noble about me is the depth of the affection and passion I feel
for you. Your talk on the phone is never chatter to me, instead I lap
up every moment, grateful for the sound of your beautiful boyish
voice, desperate to suck the tongue out of your head. I want to know
every detail of you.

Speaking of being above you physically, please don't shave your
ass or balls for a few weeks before we see each other. I want to
experience you hairy, first, and then make you submit to a careful
shaving from me, your body exposed to my hands and gaze in the
most undignified way. Once the crack of your ass is smooth and
clean, I want to be able to play with your pretty hole, probe you with
my fingers. I have been feeling the most intense desire to fuck you. I
think in part because my feelings for you have become incestuous.
You are a beautiful younger brother to me, I would do anything for
you, I want to show you how much I treasure you by fucking you
deeply and long, as any elder brother should. I want you leaning over,
your face in the crook of your arms, with your astonishingly slender
hips presented to me, my dick going in and out of you. I want you on

>144

your back, the back of your thighs pressed against me, tongues deep in each other's heads and me deep in your gut.

It's too early in the morning for this, I know, and I must try to sleep again. Will jack off thinking about reaming you. I'm glad you and Aaron may be fuck-buddies. I hope though that he doesn't burden you--don't let your natural goodness put you in the position of being bored with him, if his qualities as a top have not sufficiently developed, or if the chemistry is not right. I want only pleasure, intensity, quality jism for you. Same goes for me--that is, banish me when I bore you.

Kevin

--- ▸ ---

FROM PAUL
DATE: WEDS, MAY 1
Kevin,

I slept from eleven p.m. to almost ten a.m. this morning--more sleep than I've gotten in a month. My neck is still a bit stiff, but I hope to get out into the sun and have some warmth on it for a little while. Yesterday I did go to Blue Cut for about an hour. Not to hike, mind you, but to take my shirt off and let the sun beat on my neck. I found a rock and sat, my back to the sun, and was, at first, fairly indifferent to the little cruising that was going on around me. All in all, I did get four loads anyway. One recently divorced man with a smallish penis springing up from a tuft of red pubic hair. He complimented me on my cocksucking skills and told me that no woman could suck dick as well as a guy. Next, two Hispanic men sauntered by and both pulled their cocks out for me to service. They came very quickly and both shot enormous quantities —all over my face. I could feel the thick mass of cum beginning to move slowly down my cheeks like a jism glacier. The last was a young Chicano boy who I'd blown before, and he allowed me to work his uncut beef and slurp up his ever-flowing pre-cum before pulling my head down to the base of his dick and shooting his load against the back of my gulping throat.

Not too bad for an hour's break from schoolwork! Today I'm afraid I won't find time to search out cock, but I'm looking forward to hearing about your blowjobs yesterday. Your last post about fucking me like a younger brother nearly made me release my load in my pants yesterday--you know you can have me any way you want, and your hands, eyes, and cock can have free reign over this boy's body at your command. I only want my big brother's groans of approval as his cock slides up my asshole as far as his length will take him. Every orifice of my body is at your service, you know, and I'm eager for you to probe each one. Have fun this weekend and think of me now and then. You'll be on my mind continually.

Paul

FROM KEVIN
DATE: THURSDAY, MAY 2
Paul,

I told you yesterday that I hadn't accomplished anything but two blowjobs, one in and one out. Ray called after the usual exchange of messages. I told him he could come right over. We hadn't gone over his stats at all, but I liked his voice, and he turned out to be a good-looking masculine guy in his late 30s, tall, short dark hair with gray patches. A few silver strands in his dark pretty bush, too, once his clothes came off, and a smooth hairless olive-skinned body, well proportioned. His dick quickly turned into a fat 7" hard, a pleasure and a challenge to suck. At one point I made him lie on his side on the bed, with me kneeling on the carpet, in order for me to deep throat him in the deepest possible way. He was verbal and appreciative. His sexy talk escalated as he approached climax, a chivalrous way of warning me that he was coming, but I ostentatiously stayed on the job, and drew away only far enough to let him watch his cum spurt in and around my mouth, before swallowing him to the root again.

A dedicated cocksucker, I next met an e-mail appointment with a steady trick in downtown San Francisco. Barry is a favorite of mine. Say's he's bisexual and married, lives in the city and works as graphics guy. 35, 6'2", 200 lbs of blond muscle, 7" dick, friendly and sexy manner. Have sucked him off three or four times. Our first rendezvous was in the porn shop in Chinatown, as has been each subsequent time until this, when we met at a similar place in Polk Gulch. He is almost a creature of gay porn: handsome, smiling, untroubled countenance; bodybuilder's bulging physique of enormous chest, curves everywhere; big rock hard dick with shaved pubes and tight balls that disappear sometimes into his groin when he fucks my face. While I suck him he always rubs my shoulders in the most amiable way, while never making much of a move toward my dick—which is fine with me. I have always avidly swallowed his tasty sperm, and he has always seemed pleased. Last time we even went for coffee afterward in North Beach, which fortunately didn't break the spell: we talked about work and the rest without dispersing our interest in each other as sources of sex. When I said he

ought to pose for my camera, he said he'd need to lose some weight
first. To me he is in no way fat, but simply as sexy and burly as
the Farnese Hercules.

You, on the other hand, are as slender as the Capitoline Spinario,
a seated bronze boy leaning into his lap, removing a thorn from his
heal. How I'd like to remove that thorn with my teeth, then remove
the cum from your balls with my mouth on your cock.

Kevin

--- ▶ ---

FROM PAUL
DATE: FRI, MAY 3
Kevin,
Finished Clarissa just moments ago, and am very pleased to have
read the longest novel written in English. Logged on to 127 mes-
sages--they all came trickling in today. I'm on three or four discus-
sion lists, so they tend to pile up if not read right away.

Your post was absolutely pornographic. I sit here with my cut-
offs unbuttoned, a hard-on reaching up toward my navel. You thoroughly turn me on, Kevin, and your expert sleaziness is something
to which I can only aspire. Wish I had some juicy tale to tell you, but
it's been all drought and famine around here except for some dry
humping with Aaron. The other day I practiced deep throating him,
but my sore throat prevented me from being absolutely successful
with it. His cock is just the right size and shape for my mouth, however, so I have hopes for future assays.

Santa Monica was wonderful today--bright and breezy with just
enough passersby to make the promenade interesting, without being

overbearing. West Hollywood was, as always, very white, very body-oriented, very attitude-flinging; but I did get some badly needed sunglasses. Drank too much coffee, but I'm going to try to hit the hay anyway.

Loved hearing your voice again today--you'll never know how much you soothe me when we talk. Can hardly wait to see you--only 13 days to go! Hopefully I'll be in some acceptable state for your ravishings, but laying eyes on you again will be reward enough. I love you, Kevin, and am thirsty for your sweet, thick cum. I'm licking my lips now....

Good night, my charmer,
Paul

--- ▶ ---

FROM PAUL
DATE: SAT, MAY 4
Kevin,
My throat has been feeling a lot better today, and I have hopes for its recovery soon. Aaron and I actually had a nice session of my deep-throating him this morning. Wish I could just turn the volume down on my gag reflex, though. I guess some men think it's sexy.

Hope you are well, happy, and cock-satisfied. I'm so looking forward to seeing, touching and sucking you.

Oh I nearly forgot! Tomorrow I'm going into LA to be in a very short video on bathroom sex that a UCLA film student is making. Reliable sources told him I'd be perfect for the job, so now I'm going to utilize my tearoom sensibilities for the sake of art. I'll tell you all about it when I'm back. I'm also planning to go to a Tom of Finland

Foundation party afterward, so that should be fun.

Now I'll sign off. Go wild this weekend, and give me every delicious detail. Suck a few for me.

Love,

Paul

--- ▶ ---

FROM KEVIN

DATE: MONDAY, MAY 6

Paul,

Sorry to hear about your throat problems. Hope it's better soon,
soon. Don't worry about being in less than top form when you come
up, you will be my delight in any condition, though of course I want
you to be free of all discomfort and unhappiness. Seems most unjust
that we can't always be the happy meat-machines of sexual fantasy
and pornography, always ready for action, impervious to all injury.
As a boy reading my father's copy of the Marquis de Sade, I was
struck by the unrealistic ways in which Justine was sexually tor-
mented--even cast into a pit of corpses--but then was always
instantly fresh and pretty for her next mortification. In the same
way I still believe (irrationally, intuitively) that a post-orgy shower
restores virginity and that a stick of gum expunges all trace of
cock and ass.

Now, Venus I have served better in the last few days, or at least
Aphrodite Porne. After photo group I went off to suck on little
Michael's enormous blond dick for an hour or so. I know we'll stay in
touch (in fact, I have an idea for a couple of shots of him), but he
is exhausting. His dick is too big. I tongue-fuck his ass until my jaw

hurts. He makes me work for his load.

Yesterday was a banner day, three new tricks. After a wholesome early afternoon with a best-buddy at an elegant restaurant party-- enjoying free food, speaking French with little old ladies and jokey waiters--arrived at home of Mitchell in a bad neighborhood of once splendid Victorian row houses. He was dissapointing: half-Japanese-- which I normally love--but too Daruma-like in the face (a great sage, but not a sex object), and tending to fat. He hustled me into his squalid room, like a hundred other SF bedrooms I have seen: blocked-up fireplace, old paint on wood trim, ashtrays for ciga- rettes and incense. As we got started he changed the music to an old Roxy Music CD: a perfect choice, intelligent and sensual. I wasn't enthusiastic but also didn't stint in my attentions to his dick, and flipped around soon enough to offer him my own bigger hard-on. He sucked me eagerly and well. There followed a very nice half hour of hypnotized cocksucking. He asked me how I wanted him to cum, I said: How about down my throat? He wanted me to come too, but I told him I had a date later.

In a big step up the ladder of socioeconomic class and conven- tional beauty, I found Dave in his attractive, well-ordered condo on one of the city's mountaintops. 34, 5'11", 165 lbs, soft short straight dark hair, clean-shaven, wholesome intelligent face with a touch of the Mediterranean (one Jewish grandparent, he later divulged). Just the kind of handsome young man who is the despair of nice young heterosexual women and their marriage-minded mothers. After a glass of water and a perfectly nice chat, I told him I felt a little wrecked by a long day in record-breaking heat and a little intimi- dated by his good looks. Suggested there would be no hard feelings if he wanted to send me packing. He laughed in a boyish way and said, no, he wanted to proceed. So I plunged my face, as usual, into the lap of his jeans as he sat on his white leather couch, and began to run my hands under his shirt. He had fair skin with a lovely fan of dark hair over his stomach and chest, big tender nipples. I pulled his jeans off to reveal a beautiful, already hard, maybe 7" cock in whorls of glossy dark brown hair. He moaned approvingly as I sucked and licked his heavy lolling balls, then began to work his very smooth fat dick. Got it almost all the way down facing him, then shifted around so that I could get his up-curved member completely to the thick root, to his enthusiastic groans. Made him stand up so I could watch him loom over me as my mouth massaged his cock and I pulled little tastes of pre-cum out of him. I loved seeing his chang-ing expression, his eyes closed, from that vantage. Flat on his back again, he fairly jumped with pleasure when I moved down his per-ineum to lick his hairy hole. I made my tongue a cock and fucked him as long and as hard as I could. Each thrust registered in his body and on his face, because even with my tongue deep in his ass-hole I could see past his towering shaft to his distant face. So intense were his responses that I came up for air just long enough to say that I wanted his load when he shot. When he did cum, seated with me kneeling before him, he was racked with spasms as my mouth filled with his sperm. I didn't want to overdo it—so many guys are super sensitive on cumming—but I also didn't want to lose a drop. So I swallowed his load and held his cock deep in my throat for its final throbs, withdrawing smoothly and carefully when his shuddering had almost entirely ceased. His pretty dick was still hard when he pulled his pants on many minutes later, and we parted with a handshake and a hug.

Last stop, another huge step up the class-and-money scale; no longer the good college/good taste/good job world of Dave, but instead the inherited-boodle or self-made-millionaire world of Felix: 39, 6', 165 lbs, very short hair flecked with gray, European father, Polynesian mother, handsome in a brooding, shrewd way. Showed me through foyer into his dimly lit living room, glimpses of other rooms, every corner designed to death with precious, useless objects displayed in museum--or designer showroom--fashion, under art-fully placed spots. I know I sound bitchy, and admit that part of this is envy. But it seemed unreal, a stage set, contrived; there were big asymmetrical swags of drapery everywhere. Then, outside his windows, the most perfectly framed expanse of SF panorama I have ever seen, from Golden Gate on the far left, through Alcatraz, Coit Tower and downtown on far right.

But down to work. He asked me to proceed as I wanted, I told him I hoped he would tell me what he liked. Smooth dark skin, very muscular, Incan stonework butt--that is, tightest possible ass crack. I mouthed him through his workout shorts, and pulled them off to find his hard dick in a clean but almost-destroyed jockstrap. I pulled one shaved testicle and then the other out of the patch, then sucked him at length through the disintegrating cloth. His dick wasn't huge, but was hard and tasty. He loved having the glans licked and sucked, so I loved doing that. He offered me poppers, which I declined, and realized he was, indeed, popping them--so they were the real thing, not the bottled stuff available to regular folk. He came standing up, jacking himself toward my mouth, after making me groan that I wanted to take his load. I love that moment, that suspense, just before a man shoots his cum out of his swollen dick into my waiting mouth. Tossing himself back on the couch, he said he'd sleep well that night. I told him I hoped we'd repeat the experience.

Forgot to tell you about my Monday night, for Chrissake. Met, for the first time, a research fellow at UC whose accent I couldn't place...Iberian? Polish? Turned out to be a 36-year-old Hungarian, 6'2", 180 lbs, brown hair and eyes. A nice-looking guy, with a modest boy-next-door expression. Perhaps because his tidy bedsit had no sofa on which to exchange pre-coital conversation, I didn't lose any time dropping to my knees and nuzzling his crotch. Soon I had his pants down and his chubby uncut dick in my mouth. Moved to the bed, where he pulled off my clothes as I undressed him, and rolled around exploring his nice but unathletic body. As I sucked him I turned around on my side to let him pull vigorously on my hard dick. Though clearly interested in my boner, he said he hoped I didn't mind, but he wasn't so much for sucking dick himself. I assured him with a smile that it wasn't a problem. He warned me not too much later that I should slow down or he would cum, but then he came immediately anyway. Because I was sucking on his balls at the moment, most of his jism splashed, wasted, on his belly but I got the last of it in long deep strokes in my mouth. I left him not long thereafter, after a brief friendly exchange in which he admitted that this was his first blowjob from a man, though he had been with a guy once before. He called the next day saying he wanted to get together again, next time not so rushed.

This brings up the interesting subject of virgins: what fun it is to be a guy's first sexual experience with a man, and the responsibility of doing a good job, to show him what he's been missing and that maybe nobody sucks dick better than a fag. More soon. Welcome back. I'll call you tonight.

    Kevin

--- ▶ ---

FROM KEVIN
DATE: TUESDAY, MAY 7
Paul,

My dear lad, thank you for your latest note. Glad your throat is better, and trust that you'll be fully yourself again soon. Delighted that you'll be exhibiting your public sex expertise for the camera, but who is this reliable source that recommended you? I guess some lights won't be hidden under a bushel. I've always wanted to put "cocksucker" near the top of my CV, but for now will have to rely on word of mouth. And advertising.

    Just returned from an eleven p.m. date. Hopped on the bike and tooled through quiet Berkeley streets and across dream-like campus. Albert turned out to be very short, early 30s, looking in the face vaguely like a Velasquez or Goya subject. Perhaps it was his de rigueur goatee. Sometimes I think if I see one more little beard I will commit mass murder. This does not apply, of course, to the wonderful Pharaonic/Amish chin whiskers you had when I met you. Yours were not the standard-issue facial arrangement that every man of fashion insists on wearing this year. And you are handsome enough to wear any bon chic and remain de bon genre.

    Van Dyke or no, I blew him. His dick was slender, longish, and hard--that is, the skin of his cock when erect was taut, making him seem harder still. I sucked him as he stood, as he sat, and when we moved to his bed, where we were soon 69ing enthusiastically. He eagerly ate my asshole, so I briefly reciprocated. Finally I returned to my wonted subordinate position and pumped him with my hand, sucking his glans, until he came in my mouth.

The last two days I've been obsessing again about publishing our correspondence. I've gone through hundreds of porn images from my vast stash, cutting up 70s and 80s images, mostly from European magazines, to use as illustrations. My worry at the moment is that it will be unwieldy; there is so much text already, and now I'm mentally formulating pages of text with dirty pictures.

Enjoy LA, know I'll be thinking of you, wishing you all pleasures, and sending you my abiding love.

Kevin

--- ▸ ---

FROM PAUL
DATE; TUES, MAY 7
Kevin,
Thought I'd just reiterate my experiences of yesterday--for posterity, of course.

I asked Aaron to come along since there was a Tom of Finland foundation party (i.e. leather crowd) going on in Hollywood, and I knew that he had just bought a pair of chaps that needed breaking in. We got into LA on time, but good old Max was hung over (actually he was still drunk), so he kept us from arriving at the UCLA restroom shoot on time. Philip had a permit for shooting the film, and we felt bad about all the legitimate cruisers who were turned away from enjoying their favorite tearoom.

For the most part the filming was tedious and difficult. My scenes were mainly uninteresting except for one in which I poke a flaccid cock through the glory hole, and another where Philip's drop-dead gorgeous boyfriend sucks on my cock through the hole. (My cock entered his mouth at half-mast, but emerged throbbing.) We finished up at four, and headed to the T of F party.

The party was great--lots of bad art, but some wasn't bad at all. Very interesting crowd of all kinds of people. Saw a slave hanging from wrist restraints and rope from the rafters, a great homocore band, a series of floggings, and a fairly gruesome episode of auto-erotic self-mutilation. Scott O'Hara was there as well as a few other notables, and Aaron was thrilled to be surrounded by so many dad-dies. Every once in a while he'd shout "You're fucking hot, Sir!"

Then we headed to the Faultline, which was OK, but not near as sleazy as we all wanted. Max and I talked a long time about gay male health and all the nasty business that we boys put up with to make one another writhe in libidinal ecstasy. We're a collective of veritable martyrs, we are.

Then on to Cuffs for some real action. Aaron immediately found his element and got in trouble over and over for doing all the wrong things, while I found a far too sadistic top who slapped my balls silly with his belt, poured a bottle of water down the front of my pants, and then had me jerk him off--all over the front of my pants. Afterwards, he pulled out my shirt-tails and wiped his cock clean. I'll have to admit, I was totally turned on by that final touch of absolute disdain. Then I was introduced to Principal Don--a very large man with a thick wooden paddle who pulled my pants down to my ankles and spanked me in front of an appreciative crowd. Next another older gentleman sidled up for some spanking action, so my ass got well used for a while.

As Aaron was almost thrown out of Cuffs (you have to be pretty bad to get booted out of that place), we decided we needed to head home.

Of course, that left me pent-up like a fucking volcano, so today, cruising was a big priority--but more about that tomorrow.

I loved hearing your voice tonight and got a thrill about hearing the first stages of our published adventures. I'm all for the various levels of anxiety and nervousness this publication of my personal propensities will raise, and totally trust your taste and judgment in the actual layout of the thing. I can't wait until we are side by side working on the project together.

Sleep well, my prince, and I'll write to you again soon.

Paul

--- ▶ ---

FROM PAUL

DATE: WEDS, MAY 8

Kevin,

Aaron and I have just had a long talk about HIV and safe sex. He began to make me a little upset because he told me that he felt as though he couldn't, with any peace of mind, suck on my cock or have my semen on him. I asked him if he kept these standards for his encounters with strangers, and he said no, but he knew that it was irrational and a double standard. I understand that there is very little that is rational about sexual desire and behavior, but I was beginning to feel singled out and sort of like a pariah. I told him so, and suggested he decide what his standards of safe sex were and then stick to them across the board. I really don't care if he ever sucks my cock, but I hate knowing that he's afraid of me on some level. I've grown very fond of him, and want to continue to see him, but I can't be feeling like a contagious agent either. I think he understands and is sympathetic to my views--in fact he agrees with me on a rational level. I'm happy he was honest about how his decisions about safe sex have been irrational and inconsistent, and I know he really will consider his stance more carefully, but it still hurt a little. I hate being made to bear the burden of this epidemic, even by those who should know better and should be making real efforts to ease that burden--but we're all victims of this stupidity, I guess, and I really can understand his paranoia. Aaron used to be so freaked out about HIV that he wouldn't deep kiss for a long time (this was a long time ago--not with me), and I know he's working through a certain amount of hypochondria. Anyway--I thought I'd just vent here for a minute.

So on Monday I went to the canyon and had a great success. Man #1 was a father figure who pulled his car to the side of the road just as I drove up, and I got out to talk to him. He had wet spots on the front of his shorts and was obviously aroused, so I reached in and squeezed his cock. He pulled it out and it was a nice dripping uncut specimen that needed some attention. He asked me to take my shirt off and my pants down, and show him my body--right there on the side of the road, so of course I was happy to oblige. Exciting to be naked in the open with all the attendant possibilities of being surprised by unsuspecting passers-by. I began to suck his cock through his fly and without any warning he allowed some of his piss to trickle out, and I made approving moaning noises. He immediately

reached into his car and gulped down an entire large bottle of miner-
al water in record time, and after a while he was muttering "ye ah,
drink that hot stream of piss!" as he let loose down my throat. It
was VERY hot, and it drove me to distraction.

Soon we had a visitor--a young Hispanic man who walked over
with his hard-on sticking out of his fly, and I took turns sucking them
both. My piss daddy wanted me to take his load on my face, but just
as he came, a car pulled up too closely, and we had to scamper a bit-
-I was naked except for a jockstrap. The Hispanic guy left, and I went
back to the daddy's cock. He gave me a little more piss, and then
pulled out to pump his load all over my face. He came big and thick,
and when I stood up and saw my sloppy face reflected in his car window, I thought, "If only Kevin could be here in front of me now !"

The next batch of tricks was less exciting, but I enjoyed sucking
on them nonetheless. Man #2 had a thick, stout piece of meat that I
sucked until he shot his wad all over my face and mouth. I licked my
lips and then allowed his cock to rest in my mouth until he went soft.
Man #3 was a very nervous married type whom I'd sucked before. He
was panicking about a helicopter that was passing overhead, but
once I reassured him, he let me suck on him until he burst. It didn't
take him long at all, and I was happy for a quick load.

Contestant #4 was another fellow I'd sucked on previously, and
he had all sorts of sexual stamina going for him. His cock was also
short and thick, and he loved ramming his meat into my face, my
front teeth clicking against a metal cock ring around his dick and
balls. He also christened my face with his cum, and I then dropped my
own surprisingly and disappointingly small load before heading home.

But Monday's adventures don't stop there.... That night I logged onto the BBS. I've told you about and began to talk to a number of very nasty men--all wanting company that night. I chose the one closest to me, and began to make plans to visit him. He lived about 20 minutes away, and although it was one a.m., I decided to go over and suck him for a while. He was a large bisexual man, not extraordinarily attractive by any standards, and his cock was nothing to jump and shout about either. He liked to lie on the couch, watch straight porno, and have me suck or jerk his cock, which kept a steady rhythm of becoming alternately hard and soft. After an hour of this, I decided I was bored, although he was a very good talker--except for those moments when he suggested that, since my mouth was so good for sucking cock, I ought to try eating pussy. There is simply not one heterosexual or bisexual bone in my body. When I made gestures of leaving he asked me to wait and made me lie down on a sheet he'd spread on the floor. He then sat upright and began to piss all over my chest and groin--a very nice surprise that made the evening more interesting. Then I came (again a miniscule load) and told him good night. He suggested I come over sometime and service his buddies, and I told him I'd give him a call.

And then yesterday I made an appointment to meet with a leather top in Costa Mesa this Saturday. He is very interested in dressing me in leather and paddling me, and has other "surprises" in store. Aaron has been with him once, and told me he is fun and respectful of limits. However, he insisted I play with myself lots this week without cumming, and although I certainly don't HAVE to obey him, I think it would be kind of fun to build up an impressive load for Saturday. So I'll try to oblige.

So there's my week so far! Nice and eventful after a brief hiatus.

>d.o.c.

I've downloaded an image viewer from the BBS and a number of very nice cum shots--so when you are here, I'll have to show you my new collection.

Hope you are well and satiated with sex. I'm so looking forward to our week, and to seeing you. I'm also still thinking about aliases, but haven't stumbled across anything particularly meaningful. The more I think about your suggested title Drunk on Cum, the more I like it...and want to be it!

Hope to hear from you soon--take care, my fellow cum-sucker, and think of me as the next load hits the back of your throat.

Paul

 --- --- ---

FROM KEVIN

DATE: THURSDAY, MAY 9

Paul,

I think I have to begin paste-up process of our nasty adventures. I have begun dreaming, almost alarmingly, of page layouts. What pseudonym do you want to use? How big a document do you think you can receive by e-mail? I could send you back your earliest posts to change names.

As for cock, I have two incidents to report. Saw the young Hungarian scientist for the second time last night. Making real progress, our virgin deigned to suck my dick and stick his tongue up my ass. Don't mean to be arch, it was sexy and touching, but there was something--his pheromones, I don't know--that left me detached about our lovemaking. Perhaps that's what I mean: love-making. I did my best to give him the romantic sex that he wanted, with lots of kissing (another step) and caresses, but he isn't enough my type, I think, to continue. Even so, he came in my mouth after an hour and a half of sucking and stroking.

Today had a guy named Greg, who turned out to be a dud. Early 30s, shortish, baldish, fattish, and with the usual goddamned little beard. Sheesh. I could have sent him home but didn't. At least he was a good sport about sucking my dick proficiently when I moved around to 69. There is something there about relative status: when the man in front of me is not particularly beautiful, or aggressive, or big-dicked or hard-dicked, it prompts me to make him recipro-cate. OK fatboy, suck. No, of course I didn't say that. I just scooted around and stuck my hard dick in his little beard, and felt on the verge of cumming the entire time.

So I'll send this and phone you, hope I find you in. Miss you miss you miss you.

Kevin

--- ▶ ---

FROM PAUL
DATE: FRI, MAY 10
Kevin,

I'm looking forward to my "training" this weekend--of course I'll tell you all about it.

Yesterday I did have a nice afternoon of cocksucking at the park. Went in the afternoon, and usually I never go then. Walked into the most promising bathroom, locale-wise, and immediately two guys came in looking for action. Both were Latino, one husky, bearded, with a fat mushroom-head cock, the other boyish with two hoop earrings and a more average sized and shaped prick. Both were uncut. I alternated sucking on the two, and the hefty boy was the first to blow. While I slid my head up and down on his thick slippery shaft, he threw his head back and groaned "I'm cumming" and I swallowed. Moved over to the boyish cock, and sucked him until he began to jerk himself off. Kept my mouth at the top of his dick so I could catch his sperm on my tongue as he watched himself spurt into my mouth. Immediately another beautiful Latino boy came in. His cock pointed right to the ground while he was erect, but it was lengthy and also uncircumcised. It actually fit very nicely into my mouth and down my throat, and I was happy to bypass the gag reflex for once. I sucked him only for a few minutes before he became rigid with anticipation, and I swallowed his cock to the hilt, feeling it pulse while he shot his jism deep into my throat. I didn't even taste a drop.

Since my luck was so good yesterday, I tried for a repeat performance today, and was even more successful. Cock #1 was that of a Mexican immigrant who hardly spoke English--he filled his white briefs nicely, and had an immense cock considering he couldn't have been more than 5'6" and 135 lbs. He was very appreciative of my sucking abilities, and was thrilled when I kept my mouth at his piss-slit to catch every drop of his semen when he shot. It even dripped out of the corner of my mouth à la porno stories, and he had to remind me to lick the drips back into my mouth.

Next I followed a white, middle-aged, and very fit man down a trail I'd never seen before where he removed his T-shirt and walked into a small cove of foliage. He let me suck his lengthy, curving cock, but didn't want to shoot into my mouth or on my face. He said he was married and needed to be careful, and despite the confused logic, I convinced him to unload on my chest. As he beat himself off, he kept warning me "I cum a lot, so just be prepared." "Not enough for me," I responded, hooking my T-shirt over the back of my neck to give him a clear target. As per his warning, he came in buckets, and it all pooled in an impressive puddle in my pubes. I had nothing to wipe it off with, so I merely wiped it all over my torso, as he thanked me and left.

Toying with the idea of leaving, I drove around the park once more hoping for just one more trick, and found a young Hispanic hitchhiker. I pulled over and asked him what was up, and he said "just cruising," so I asked him where we could go so I could su ck on him. He suggested the trail to the foliage again, so back I went, and sucked down another load from a pretty, uncut, perfectly shaped and sized cock. He confessed he had run out of gas, so I took him to a gas station to get a canister and a couple of gallons, and then back to his car.

Finally I decided it really was time for me to go, but as I drove past the trailhead, I saw another beautiful young thick-thighed youth in athletic shorts and a tank top walking down the tell-tale trail. So of course I parked and followed him. He went much further than I had gone with the other two, and I was just about to give up, when he glanced my way, and ducked into smaller path crowded thickly with trees and bushes. We confronted one another a few yards into the trees, and immediately he started to grope my crotch. I told him I'd love to suck him off, so we found a small, private clearing where he ordered me to get naked. I did, and he took the belt off my pants and told me he wanted to spank my ass. As an aside, he told me to tell him when it was too hard, but I enjoyed the whipping at the hands of this strapping youth. He also had an uncut

>165

dick which oozed lots of pre-cum, so I spent a good time creating
ropes of ooze that bridged my lips and tongue to his prepuce. After
nearly an hour of my sucking him, rimming his tight, freshly-
scrubbed butthole, and being spanked and whipped, I asked for his
piss. I got to my knees, and kept my mouth open, while he concentrated fervently on his bladder. He was only able to produce a drib-
ble, but I swallowed it and then told him I wanted his load, and,
jerking himself, he quickly shot onto my extended tongue.

And now I'm home and smelling like sex. The three-way you've
planned sounds great. I'm willing to have you direct me to all the
cocks you like, Kevin. The more the merrier. Just be sure I get to
your cock too.

I'm horny as hell, and can only think of sex since I'm harboring a
four-day load now. I can't wait for tomorrow morning--if only to
explode! Have a good Friday night, and I'll write to you again soon.

Paul

--- ▶ ---

FROM KEVIN
DATE: LATE SUNDAY, MAY 12
Paul,
A phone call from Pacific Heights boy. He is now so enthusiastic
about entertaining both of us at once that he wants to put us up
while you're here for an ongoing sex party. Could be fun, but I felt
my sense of control of our time together slipping away. He is a firm
young man, part of his appeal, but I don't know that I want him to
redefine your visit as a threesome, when I've so long looked forward
to it as a twosome with a supporting cast of dozens. Anyway, a full

night of sex with him will be great fun, and he's into venturing out to a sexclub or porn theater too.

Before and after talking to him--which included his reading me his account, written when it occurred at 17, of losing his virginity to a humpy 35-year-old friend of the family and pater familias-- had to say no to two promising tricks whom I'd encouraged to call late tonight. Disappointment in their voices. Hate to be a prick tease. Didn't feel up to sneaking someone into the house.

Just after talking to you today on the phone, jumped on my bike to hit the dirty bookstore. Couldn't believe my luck: just as I was tying up my steed outside, a very handsome guy in business dress came out as if to leave, looked meaningfully in my direction, and reentered the store. Wasted no time inside either, as we confirmed our mutual interest with split-second looks over the token machine. In the booth, I had a second to admire his John Kennedy, Jr. or Baldwin boys good looks: early 30s I'd say, dark brown medium length straight hair, blue eyes, clean-shaven, nice jaw. Dressed expensively in dress shirt, tie, and slacks. A studly gay guy, or an urbane straight one? Either way, very receptive to my hands and then my mouth on the bulge in his trousers. Soon I was on my knees, his pants half down, his big hard dick in my mouth. Could just get all of him in, tried to show my appreciation with avid sucking and slurp- ing. He was perfectly butch and friendly throughout, asking me if I liked his cock, telling me to lick his balls. I felt around, with some amazement, his tanned and well-formed torso, lightly bristling with dark hair, his tight round butt, his solid thighs. He reached down and pulled on my dick, said he wanted to see me jack off with his dick in my mouth. After I'd been sucking him at length while he sat,

he signaled me to stand. I wiped the head of my dripping cock with a
shirt–tail, as it pointed, twitching, at his face. A nice visual memory: fine neck and high cheekbones above a starched white shirt,
then his pulling me closer to him, leaning in to take my erection in
his mouth. As much as I enjoyed this, I would have been abashed to
have him suck me for long, and returned soon to fellating him.
After some time he made a move to pull up his pants and said he
would take a break ("take a break" is THE correct expression in the
argot of American anonymous sex for breaking off contact before
climax, yes?), when I looked up and asked him if he didn't want to
jack off in my face. He said he would if I thought I could jack myself
off at the same time. So he did and I did. Assumed he wouldn't let
me take his load, but I enjoyed spreading his copious cum all over
my parted lips, as he protected his pants by catching the overflow
in his left hand. I shot on the floor at his feet and produced a clean
handkerchief (cocksucker's blue) to let him wipe off. He waited a
moment patiently while I scrambled to write him my name and number. He won't call, but I like to leave that unlikely little door open,
just in case.

How many dozens of business cards have I handed to men I've
just sucked off? I imagine most of them meeting the same fate as
that of prissy old Adolph Menjou's calling card on being accepted
cordially by Marlene Dietrich in the film Morocco: torn into little
pieces and flicked into the sea. But you never know.

Love,

Kevin

 --- ▶ ---

FROM KEVIN

DATE: SUNDAY, MAY 12

Paul,

So you've been disciplined today. Hope you had a good time. Just returned from a party, didn't know many people there, but had a fine time anyway. Had plenty of wine. Lots of intelligent Berkeley straight people of a certain age.

But my real news: saw a sexy guy yesterday or the day before from AOL. Doug, early 30s, extremely tight athletic body, appealing sweet-butch face. Big nose, rough skin, bright eyes and perceptive expression. Dragged him into the bedroom, got his clothes off to reveal a dynamite body. Didn't have the house to ourselves, as I'd hoped, so a certain amount of slurping and sucking went on while George returned a call down the hall. I was sucked by him happily, and his muscular lean blond body had at its center a very nicely formed 7" erection, neither too fat nor too thin, which tasted great and went down the throat pretty well. He was friendly and open, and after a while I responded to his cues by shedding the rest of my clothes and climbing onto the bed with him for a nice languid session of mutual sucking. As usual, I felt touched by this, and appreciated his nice boyish face swallowing my hard dick. Eventually though I switched around to take his dick in my mouth in the accustomed straight-on stance, and sucked and hand-pumped him toward climaxing in my face. (Did MFK Fisher have this problem, describing a delicious new meal in a way that would distinguish it from the last delicious meal? When half the cast—me—remains the same, and the activity is the usual cocksucking and cum-eating, is tedium inevitable?) Like a good boy, he announced he was about to cum. Like a bad boy, I moaned and muttered my approval, positioned myself to take his load. It was copious and delicious.

Went today, in another unexpected heat wave, to the Castro for window shopping and boy gawking. Looked at the 'zines at A Different Light. Will they really carry something as profane as I foresee? Back in the East Bay, stopped by my neighborhood dirty bookstore. Immediately caught the eye of a Hispanic or Arab boy in his early 20s, cute, short, furry, sweet-faced, ready for fun. He joined me in a booth without any self-consciousness, and was affectionate and sexy as our bodies moved together. I stroked and then bit his nipples through his T-shirt, felt his stiffening basket, groped his firm round rump. A big cross hung from a chain under his shirt between his furry tits, so either Latino or Palestinian Christian. He was very turned on and desirous as I got his pants down, but signaled me that he didn't want me to suck his dick. Always accommodating, I licked his balls and respected his limits. He moaned and lifted his seated butt to my face as I worked on him. He pulled me up and toward him and licked and sucked the shaft of my hard dick in a way that gave me courage to transgress when I returned to his joint––the way he stared at the head of my dick, squeezed the shaft and pointed it toward his mouth, prompted me to lick and suck the shaft of his cock in an ever-more insistent way, avoiding the head at first, but getting closer and closer. Licked up the bulging underside––his cock was six and a half or seven inches long, dark and fat––and began to pause and flick my tongue at the forbidden piss slit. Finally I was too turned on, and thought I'd softened him up enough; I swallowed his beautiful boner. Now he was enthusiastic; moaning and riding up into my

face. He stood up and grabbed the back of my head to piston my
mouth with a long series of quick rabbit-fucks. He stroked himself
with my mouth around his cock head and my tongue at his slit, a
favorite situation for me. He wanted me to cum when he did, but I
was too greedy and thought I might score again later (I didn't). He
squeezed his load out onto the floor and held my face away from
his dick, rightly suspecting that I would have, given the chance,
gobbled him up. When he asked me: what about you, meaning: why
aren't you cumming? I realized from his voice that he was fully
assimilated second or third generation––in other words, an
adorable American queer boy. We parted with a hug.

As usual I will drift off to sleep imagining that I am stroking
your face and ass.

Kevin

--- ▸ ---

FROM PAUL
DATE: MON, MAY 13
Kevin,
It was great talking with you tonight. I'm hungry for Berkeley, for
our fuckfest, and for you.

Rather than try and give you the details of this weekends' s/m
training session, I'm going to get ready for bed, and write you
tomorrow. It was a full-on sextravaganza, and so I'll have lots to
say about it. Nevertheless, I'm tired. Aaron is also next to me--writ-
ing to his sex-master on his laptop. What a strange little relationship we have. We talked more about you tonight, since you called
while he was here. He's excited for my weekend too (although he's

jealous not to be going on the sexual rampage as well).

Well good night, dear Kevin, and more tomorrow....

Paul

--- ▶ ---

FROM KEVIN

DATE: MONDAY, MAY 13

Paul,

Just had a delicious late–afternoon snack. After trading lots of calls, a
San Franciscan named Nick stopped by for the first time. He's 35, looks
much younger, 5'10", 170 lbs, medium–short wavy light brown hair,
handsome face, wining dimpled smile. Boyish and sweet but also perfectly masculine. Under his baggy shorts and t–shirt, a furry stocky
body and fat dick and balls. Very, very attractive. Big shoulders, heavy
pecs, long solid joint. He made lots of pleased sounds as I began to
suck his dick and lick his big balls, which he or I held compact under
his shaft so they didn't ride up too much into his body. Kicked back
on the couch, he raised his hips to let me get more of him down my
throat. Said he liked that, in a husky whisper, and told me to suck his
dick. He reached down and squeezed my boner a few times. Neither of
us had much time, so I fell back on jacking him while sucking on the
head and the top half of his shaft. Want me to cum? he asked. I said:
I'd love it. Later: you're making me get close. Me: I want that load. He
moaned at this and began to erupt in sweet gouts of stuff in my
mouth. I pumped him harder with my throat and slowed down when he
did, letting, as usual, his cock rest buried in my face. When I pulled
off, I admired again his now half–hard cock and licked the last bits of
foam from the base and balls. Caught my breath with my face in his

scrotum. He stroked my hair in the friendliest way. As we dressed, made it clear how honored I was to suck him off, and that I hoped to repeat soon and often. Really hope he takes me up on it.

Yesterday entertained two others for the first time. In the afternoon a neighbor––he did look familiar when we met––who is handsome in a butch Mephisphelean way but seemed rather older than his declared 35. Remarkable bod: lanky (6'5"!), darkly tanned, thick, cut 7" rod. In person he repeated that he would like a regular stop after hitting the gym a few times a week, an after-workout reward. Sucked him to our mutual satisfaction. Swallowed every drop. He put on his clothes and helmet, shook hands, and rode off on his bike.

In early evening agreed that a certain Peter would come over. Dad of a small child; he lives in the burbs, is 34, 6'2" with a 10" dick. When he came striding up the sidewalk, was surprised and pleased to find that he was a handsome African American guy. I had a great time sucking his snaky cock, which though amazingly long was thin enough to fit all the way down my throat without any difficulty. Worked on him enthusiastically for a time until I glanced up and saw a grimace cross his face as I deep throated him. Asked if he was getting teeth, and I proceeded with greater caution. He too gave me all his sweet load. We dressed and I walked him back out to the street in the gathering darkness.

All for now. I am so happy that you will be here soon. Hope your work is going well, and I'll talk to you before Thursday.

Much love,

Kevin

--- ▶ ---

FROM PAUL
DATE: MON, MAY 13
Kevin,
So I'll begin with Saturday morning.

Master Dick is an S/M top with over 20 years of experience and
an enormous collection of leather. He is a good friend and fuck
buddy of Aaron's master. Drove to his place wearing the not-so-
clean jockstrap and sweat socks he had ordered me to wear. When
he answered the door, I was greeted by an older, satanic-looking
gentleman--not an attractive man, but I expected he would be less
appealing for his looks than for his S/M savoir faire. Immediately
directed me to his room without saying a word. Noticed his self-
made black frame bed with hooks and chains hanging from the posts
and cross-beams, and tried to take in the huge array of leather
paraphernalia, but it was simply too baroque to absorb. Was forced
down to his boots which I licked greedily, as he muttered "good
boy, good boy." Then I stripped down, and put on a pair of leather
boots he had set aside for me. He placed leather restraints around
my ankles and wrists, and then he chained me standing spread-
eagled at the foot of his massive bedstead. He used a small flogging
whip on my buttocks and thighs for a bit, and then began to stretch
my ball sack downward with his fist. He grabbed a parachute
stretcher which he placed around my balls, but first pinched a bit of
my scrotum in the snap. I flinched, and told him he'd caught me--I
began to bleed, so he rubbed medicated ointment on the small surface cut, and then secured the stretcher in place. From my perspective I couldn't see the small metal hook beneath my balls, but he
suspended what felt to be anywhere from a 5 to 10 lb. lead weight

from my balls. I expected to be in more pain, but I quickly got accustomed to having weight hanging from my genitals.

While making the lead weight sway between my legs with his thigh, Master Dick continued to flog my thighs, stomach and buttocks, and then asked me if I wanted to taste his cock. I begged him for a taste of his dick, and my own cock stiffened quickly, as he released my arms. On my knees with my ankles stretched back toward his bed, I sucked on his large, uncut cock while he inched his way backward, causing me to stretch forward, tongue extended hoping to taste more of his dripping foreskin.

But this was short-lived, because he then placed me flat on my back on the bed, and once again spread my limbs in four directions and fastened them to chains and hooks. In this position he worked my cock with various strong oils that caused a burning sensation along the shaft. He insisted on rubbing the head of my penis with his oily palm, which caused me to writhe in pleasure/pain, and nearly sent me through the roof.

Next he donned a rubber glove and fingered my asshole, eventually sliding three fingers inside me. Then he promised me a special treat--something even Aaron hadn't yet experienced. But first he placed a leather hood over my head, and covered the eye holes with a blindfold. I felt him applying goop to several spots around my groin, felt him placing some light objects on each spot, and then he turned the little gadget on. It was an electronic device--something I immediately sensed as I felt voltage vibrating through my crotch. He raised the voltage little by little, and with each increase, I felt as though I couldn't stand the new dosage, but then rather quickly adjusted to the new level of sensation. He allowed me to tell him

when the sensation was too intense--which I told him when I felt as
though I could no longer handle the extraordinary vibrating and pulsing sensations.

He changed the electrodes to new spots, and began the process
over. Once again I felt as though I had reached my limit of tolerance,
and asked him to turn the voltage down, but suddenly I felt the voltage increase drastically. I bolted upright, yanking on the chains with
my arms and legs and began to shout at the top of my lungs "It's
hurting me!" I yelled repeatedly. Baffled at my violent reaction, he
responded "But I turned it off." Well, he had turned the dial t he
wrong way, and rather than turning the contraption off, he had
turned it on full force. He quickly switched the device off, and I
spent the next five minutes hyperventilating while he hugged me and
stroked my hooded head. I doubt he had ever used the little thing at
full voltage before.

I was a little upset, but realized he had made a mistake--albeit a
fairly serious one, so he put the dreaded little machine away.
Funny, but in retrospect I kind of like the thing--once I got used to
it, it could be really erotic!

He then tied a rope to my ball sack, and stretched the rope to the
foot of the bed, where he fastened it, taut, to hook at the foot of
the footboard. Then he knelt near my head and directed me to suck
on his cock while he tugged on the ropes, stretching my balls further toward the foot of the bed. I kept sucking on him while he
stroked my cock, until he muttered: "Do you want this load on y our
chest or down your throat?"

"My mouth, Sir," I begged, and he pointed his shooting cock
into my mouth and unloaded his jism in me. Then he stroked me off

(my first load in five days!) and I shot over my head. Once we had both cum, he unfastened me and talked about S/M for the next 30 minutes. He told me I was a good first timer, but that he had three other boys who came over regularly and took enormous amounts of pain and abuse without flinching. I don't know that I really aspire to that level of self-abnegation, but I did enjoy the experience despite his occasional carelessness.

It is this carelessness that would keep me from coming back, however. I am interested in S/M bottoming more, but with someone I can trust. (And a better-looking top wouldn't hurt either!)

On my leaving, Master Dick gave me a set of too-large leather boots and a ragged leather jacket. I appreciated the kind gesture, thanked him, and left.

Since I was near LA and it was still early afternoon, I decided to hit boy's town where I bought an enema bulb, a cock ring and a ball stretcher. I spent time at the various toy stores in West Hollywood, and then called a man with the handle of Thirsty who chats on the internet bulletin board I've been playing with lately. Thirsty was having a sex party that evening, and invited me to come--but with a full bladder. So I visited the Spike which was just down the street from his house, and had a couple of beers before heading to his duplex.

Thirsty is a cute little lanky computer geek with a huge appetite for piss. He wouldn't let anyone use the toilet all night long, and was forever guzzling someone's stream. To be honest, I took a handful of piss loads myself over the evening--and really enjoyed the intimacy of feeling a man's cock soften and unload another sort of man-juice in my mouth.

Early in the evening I hooked up with a very attractive, very thick man with a large, thick, veiny cock that dripped like a leaky faucet. I spent most of my time on my knees sucking his shaft, swallowing his balls, and darting my tongue in and out of his musky asshole. Since we initiated the action in the bedroom, we ended up with a sizeable and appreciative audience. I told him I wanted his load all over my face, so he obliged by dumping a large mass of semen there, and then, to my pleasant surprise, he bent over me and licked up every drop of it. The rest of the evening I spent chatting with various partygoers, drinking a occasional load of piss, and then finished off my part of the evening with a suckfest--on my knees sucking five different cocks in turn, and taking each load on my face, to everyone's satisfaction.

Today, I was given a job in Upland through the cleaning service, and was told that it was for a 19-year-old. When I arrived at his house this afternoon, I was greeted by a very husky athletic looking youth in sweat shorts and a T-shirt. He told me to undress in his room, and then told me to clean the kitchen floor and vacuum the living room. While I did these chores, he sat on a couch and, while watching bad porno, stroked his thick cock. When I finished the floors, which had only taken me about forty-five minutes to do, I asked him what he wanted me to do next. He began to stroke my leg, and so I fell to my knees and sucked his thick meat into my mouth, giving him some serious head. He moaned in appreciation, and every so often thrust his hips upward to sink his cock even deeper in my throat. He also sucked on my cock a little, but I quickly fell to my knees and resumed sucking his. He brought me so close that, though I tried not to explode, I shot streams of cum across his chest and stomach anyway. Then I stroked his balls and kissed his lips while encouraging him to orgasm. He shot over his shoulder and coated the couch, and then, quite perfunctorily, asked how much he owed me. I told him, he paid me, and I left his house.

On the way home I bought two large jockstraps at a sporting goods store--one swimmer's strap with a very thin waistband, and another regular, but buff colored, number. I'll bring them to Berkeley with me. I'll just wear jockstraps and cock rings all weekend!

I love you, Kevin, and am counting the moments before we're together this week.

Paul

--- ▸ ---

FROM KEVIN
DATE: WEDNESDAY, MAY 15
Paul,

So, I've had my hair cut, my teeth cleaned, and taken care of most of my pre-Paul errands. I'm as ready as I'll ever be. Worry plenty when I catch my reflection in a window or mirror. My hair is grayer and my cheeks craggier every day. A rather knocked-around guy will be meeting you at the airport tomorrow. That doesn't mean I'm any less intent on greeting you with a sloppy kiss and dragging you into the nearest men's room.

Your account of your S/M encounter made me sit up in terror and suspense. No permanent damage allowed! My testicles ached in sympathy, and I wonder that he didn't knock out your short-term memory with that little black box. Besides, anybody with that kind of power over a youth as beautiful as you ought to be handsomer (and more responsible) than he sounded. A harsh master I can grant you, but one worthy of you.

Been poring over ideas for our publication. Don't know if a big self-published novel would be best, ending about now: a cliffhanger that would bring the reader to the brink of our reunion. Or would several chapbooks be preferable? The first has the advantage of a natural arc: meeting, corresponding, meeting (almost) again. After all, we have so much text now that staples won't hold it, even without images, in a single volume--unless we venture into something like real bookbinding, with signatures and glue, which could be very nice but is likely to be expensive.

I don't know what to call myself yet--Kevin perhaps, or Keith. Something common and normal, like my own name, but not among the first-rank saints' names. I wonder if our two voices in the text should be represented by different fonts, or one Roman and the other Italic? I know all this must sound--will sound--ridiculous to a third party: who are these guys that they package their affair almost before it occurs? Who run to their desktop as soon as the dick is out of their mouth? Fuck 'em. Life is too short. Might as well make it our own true-life epistolary novel.

I should send this off and try to sleep.

Much love, as ever,

Kevin